NICKERS

Robert T. Price

Constable · London

First published in Great Britain 1998
by Constable & Company Ltd
3 The Lanchesters, 162 Fulham Palace Road
London W6 9ER
Copyright © 1998 by Robert T. Price
The right of Robert T. Price to be
identified as the author this work
has been asserted by him in accordance
with the Copyright, Designs and Patents Act 1988
ISBN 0 09 478610 0
Set in Palatino 10 pt by
SetSystems Ltd, Saffron Walden, Essex
Printed and bound in Great Britain
by MPG Books Ltd, Bodmin, Cornwall

A CIP catalogue record for this book
is available from the British Library

To my wife Grace, for the wonder years

To Kate Dunn, who made me think I could write

Prologue

The phone rang, and I cursed. I had just passed the top of Bordon Hill, and was coasting down into Stratford-on-Avon, which at that time of night had a kind of orange glow hanging over it from the street lights. The sound of the phone annoyed me, because it meant that my usual careful attention to detail had slipped a bit. Normally when I nick a car, I check for a phone, and make sure it's switched off. This time, I just plain forgot. Anyway, I reached down intending to snuff out the noise, but as I plucked the phone out of its nest, I thought what the hell, and said hello. A woman's voice said:

'May I have a word with Mr Aston, please?'

'Speaking,' I lied. That must have been the magic word, because it launched the voice into its prepared spiel.

'Good evening. My name's Mandy. I represent Somnambula Security Systems. We will shortly be opening new premises in your area, and we are making an unrepeatable offer to a small élite group of privileged potential customers. I am pleased to be able to inform you that you have been specially selected as someone of sufficient discrimination to benefit from this once in a lifetime opportunity.'

Great! I made an appointment for a representative to call on Mr Aston. He should be interested in buying some security – after all, he'd just had his new car stolen.

These big German cars are always nice to drive. This one was a BMW 735. I was finding myself driving more and more examples of this kind of transport, now that Quinn was fingering a car for me to nick nearly every week. By the time this motor's previous owner had finished his first pint, the car would be a good fifteen miles from the pub car-park where he last saw it. What's more, it would be safely stashed away, waiting to have its identity changed – and my cut would soon be on its way to the Abbey National.

As usual, my first destination was up Birmingham Road to

Tesco's car-park which tends to be pretty empty at this time of night, and not too well lit out at the farthest edges. With a lot of Teutonic smoothness, I slid into the slot next to my own car which I had taken the precaution of leaving there earlier. See, preparation is dead essential in my kind of business. I need to be able to check for any goodies that the former owner might have carelessly left lying around in the car – and to transfer them to my ownership. Working for Quinn's organisation doesn't stop me turning my hand to a bit of private enterprise. I grabbed the phone and a bunch of CDs, but couldn't see anything else worth having inside the car. So I flicked the lever that opens the boot and went round to see what loot I could find.

Something was there. I pulled back the edge of the canvas sheet that covered the boot's contents. It looked like a bundle of clothes – until I saw a hand sticking out.

Christ! For a moment there I thought I might have a dead body on my hands – and that gave me quite a turn. The last thing an honest car thief needs is to get sucked into the rubble that gathers around serious crimes. But then common sense stepped in and I realised I must be seeing a part of one of those plaster window-dressing models.

I was just starting to wonder where I could sell it when the situation suddenly slid right down the grid.

The hand moved.

What I did then was – I panicked. No, that wasn't it. Nothing as ordinary as panic can describe how I reacted. I was paralysed. I just stood there with the hairs on the back of my neck trying to crawl to safety. My spine turned to custard. My brain was so busy it was standing room only for my brain cells as they held their strike meeting.

The hand moved again. It was a left hand. I could see it clearly by the automatic boot light. I dragged my eyes away for a quick check. OK! Nobody within a hundred yards. The supermarket was closed now, and this car boot was a pond of light in the warm autumn gloom.

Then I managed to recover enough to think. Maybe some poor sod had got themselves trapped in there. A child perhaps, who would be nearly as scared as I was.

I reached down to pull the canvas cover further back, and as I did so, a figure twisted and reared up on its knees, blotting out most of the light. A right hand now came into view, and it was pointing a gun at the most precious thing in the world – my head.

1

The Spotted Cow is where it all started. See, it's really great living in a place like Stratford-on-Avon; there's so many different kinds of pubs, and most of them are useful to a professional person like me at some time or other. There are the tourist pubs, like the Dirty Duck, for instance. Tourists go there hoping to rub shoulders with famous actors from the Royal Shakespeare Company. The actors don't go there, of course.

There are nice quiet pubs like the Bell, where I like to go when I'm relaxing or fancy a quiet drink with my mate Steve. Another kind is the kiddie pub like the Green Dragon where nobody is over twenty-five, and they've all come to hear live music, usually from some incompetent but very loud local group. Then there are pubs that cater to the yuppie trade – like the Spotted Cow where it all started about six months ago.

When it comes to business opportunities, the Spotted Cow is your ideal enterprise society job centre. It's always crammed with loud would-be yuppie puppies, Mexican lager, electronic games, robot music, and disgusting snack food. Not to mention loosely attended wallets, handbags, credit cards, and car keys.

The layout's good too, from my point of view; four or five rooms all running into each other. Snooty bar staff splashing beer and insults on the customers from their trench behind a fake walnut counter – which is usually awash with spillage. Better than drinking it, I suppose.

The Spotted Cow is always jam-packed on quiz night, which is Wednesday as a rule, on account of they changed from Sundays to make way for the karaoke. I never missed quiz night in those days. This particular night I was being unobtrusive as usual, hugging a pint and hanging around not quite at the bar, and not quite away from it, if you know what I mean – just part of the furniture. I was pleased with my Top Man gear and gelled spiky hair that made me look like one of the gang. I could be heading for middle management in a Curry's superstore.

Anyway, I'd just locked on to a likely punter in a green River

Island cardigan with a cellphone stretching the pocket, when I heard my name from across the angle of the bar.

'Hiya, Kenny, how's it goin'?' The yell pierced the wall of noise from the music and the yapping customers.

I flicked my eyes that way without moving my head.

'Jesus Christ,' I groaned. 'It's Nick Pearson.' I suppose Nick Pearson is a nice enough bloke, in his own way, and at the right time. But when I'm working it's definitely the wrong time. The trouble with people like Nick Pearson is that they haven't got an education like me. He used to be a reasonably competent breaker and enterer but at this time – the Spotted Cow time, that is – I didn't know what he was up to. I just hoped he had enough brights to stay out of my hair when he saw how carefully I was ignoring him.

But it's easier to get rid of a verruca than Nick Pearson. He started elbowing his way towards me and I cringed a bit because he stood out here like Dolly Parton in a monastery. I just hoped that he would be taken for a pub entertainer since he looked kind of like an Irish folk-singer in his heavy blue jersey. I don't like to be seen associating with criminals.

'Thought I might find you here,' he said, nodding busily – an irritating habit of his. 'Can we go someplace quieter? I got a sniff of somethin' that might be right up your street.'

I sighed. What the hell! The Spotted Cow was clearly a dead horse for me that night.

We went round the corner to the Gay Dog, which Nick Pearson insisted on calling the Homosexual Hound with a lot of nodding and grinning. I hate that kind of feeble attempt at humour, so I was dead careful not to smile. I let Nick Pearson buy me a drink – a malt whisky seeing as how he was so keen to talk to me – and we found a quiet corner. Nick Pearson leaned back and took a swig of his pint. I waited.

'This is just like old times, innit, Kenny,' he said at last.

We never really were mates as such, so I couldn't think of any particularly happy times we'd shared together. I nodded, still waiting. He came at me from a different direction.

'Hey, did you hear the latest about old Nige Prentice? You'll never guess what he's been and gone and done this time. It was one night last week – Tuesday, I think it was – he only comes out the back of Dixon's carryin' a pile of video recorders –

straight into the lovin' arms of the Old Bill. No, it couldn't of been Tuesday 'cos – '

I derailed him. My mate Steve once said that if Nick Pearson can't find a bush to beat around, he'll plant one.

'Come on, Nick, you didn't drag me round here to talk about the local aristocracy. Let's get to the point.'

'Oh,' he said. 'Right! Well, there's this bloke, see. He's new round here, but he's definitely got good connections. I think he's trying to get a team together for some big job or something. Anyway, his name's Quinn, an' he's heard about you. He's looking for a driver.'

By now his black curls were bobbing up and down in time with his nods. The point that Nick Pearson eventually managed to home in on was that this Quinn would like to discuss the state of the world with me next day. So Nick Pearson was just the message boy and I was being invited to a job interview. It didn't sound like the kind of thing that turns me on.

Why would I bother to turn up for a meeting with this Quinn? His information about me wasn't so hot – bloody driver indeed. I'm no hotshot getaway driver; in fact I'm dead careful to observe all the speed limits and rules of the road at all times. A solid law-abiding citizen – that's me. I was still thinking about Nick Pearson's message while I was going up the back stairs to the maisonette. That's where Aileen and I have been living for nearly two years. In fact, I was so busy thinking about Nick Pearson's message that I clean forgot to tiptoe past old Miss Downie's door, which flew open just as I got level with it.

'They've been at it again,' she screeched at me. 'What are you going to do about it?'

She fixed her squint on me, and folded her arms. The Neighbourhood Witch, Aileen called her. She monitored every movement in our street, and she had a thing about the local kids playing in the rough grassy area behind the maisonettes.

'I'm just getting home, Miss Downie. Tell me about it tomorrow.'

Luckily, she hadn't been quick enough to bar my way, so I fled on up the stairs. While I fumbled for my key, I could still hear her:

'They almost upset my wheelie-bin tonight. Discipline, that's what they need. I blame the Channel Tunnel.'

The door slammed shut.

I had managed to remember the takeaway pizzas; pepperoni with extra hot chilli for me, and a Caribbean for Aileen. Maybe her solid common sense would help me to decide. Aileen works at Jonathan Phillips – you know, the posh shoe shop down Sheep Street – and she's dead capable at practically everything. Really, she is, in spite of what you might think about somebody who can eat a pizza with lumps of pineapple on top.

I told her all about it over our pizzas and glasses of lager.

'Mmm,' she began, through a mouthful of hot pineapple. I thought I was going to get a ... what would you call it ... you know, a reasoned assessment of the situation. But I should have known she wouldn't miss a chance to jump on her favourite nag wagon.

'I don't think being an opportunist sneak thief suits you, Kendall Madigan, you know that. It's a ... a ... a diversion of your skills, that's what it is – and it's a hand to mouth existence. Look at tonight. What did you get? Sweet bugger all, that's what.'

I groaned. It's always a dangerous sign when Aileen uses my full name. I just want to curl up in a trance till she runs out of steam.

No, that's unfair. She was dead right about my present self-employment – but I wasn't ready to admit it yet. What she really wanted was for me to get what she called 'a real job', and have a career. She hadn't mentioned the 'W' word yet, but she was getting warmed up, so I knew I wouldn't have long to wait.

She went on:

'What about trying to get your old job back at the lawn mower factory?'

'Aw, come on, Aileen,' I protested. 'You know how I feel about that. Anyway, it's not a lawn mower factory any more; they've turned it into a sodding Landscape Management Centre of Excellence. That's a dead give-away; whenever a company swaps its name for a yard of jargon, you can lay odds it's in trouble. The receivers will be in there faster than you can hot-wire a Ford Capri.'

I stopped myself. I hadn't meant to pitch in so strong. It was just the thought of that place. Five years I worked there, and I was the best damned engineer they had. They forced me out when I wouldn't take their rotten 'promotion to the management team'. Sooner or later they always want you to take responsibility – and as far as I'm concerned that usually means blame.

Bastards.

And the union was just as bad; they wanted me to join so they could force me to be treated the same as the whole herd of brain-dead incompetents who go to the factory every day to read the *Sun* to each other.

Anyway, my little bit of outrage had one good result. It made Aileen give up that line of torture.

'Can't you do something where there's no chance of getting arrested or beaten up? What about computer fraud if you're dead set on a life of crime?'

That's one of the things I really like about Aileen; she thinks there's no end to my abilities. She even goes on at me to fix up some shelves above the television to hold her collection of Reader's Digest books.

'Yeah, there's money in computer fraud, all right,' I replied, 'but it's a very specialised line. You need an awful lot of training for that – not to mention expensive equipment.'

'Well,' she said, backing off for the moment, 'there must be some other way for you to earn – or at least get your mitts round – a reasonable amount of dosh. You know, some way that would let us spend more of our evenings together.'

Now she could feel that she had left a mole to burrow in among my brain cells, Aileen changed the subject, and told me about the latest wonder man in the eventful life of Sally, Aileen's best friend.

I like Sally, but she's got chronic problems in what Aileen calls 'the trouser department'. I think she (Sally, that is, not Aileen) is just a lousy judge of men. I mean, she's drop-dead gorgeous, and she's got a body that Julia Roberts would envy; so she can get any man she wants. She just can't seem to keep them for long. If you ask me, Sally's trouble is that she's too bossy. Mind you, I sometimes think some of that bossiness rubs off on my Aileen.

Later on, in bed, just before she squirmed around into her sleeping position, Aileen delivered her verdict and, at the same time, managed to have the last word as usual.

'Why don't you go and see this Quinn person? Just out of curiosity. You've got nothing to lose. You can always say no.'

Mostly, Aileen is the anchor that keeps me moving in the right direction. But this time, as it turned out, she was herding me straight into the teeth of calamity.

2

It was a sunny morning, so I walked, which took me through the town centre. I like Stratford town centre because it's always full of relaxed people with their minds on anything but their valuables. But today I walked all the way up Henley Street without even sizing up the opportunities among the crowds of tourists and trippers milling around Shakespeare's birthplace. For once I had something else to think about.

The address I got from Nick Pearson for this Quinn took me to a part of Stratford that the tourists never see; down Anthony's Bridge Road among those abandoned factories and warehouses that have been split up into units for rent. Most of these are taken up by hopeful businessmen who've sunk their redundancy money into carpet-cleaning equipment or bouncy castles for hire. None of them seem to last very long.

The place I was looking for turned out to be a section of what was once the Pinnacle Plastics factory. A recently painted sign identified it as 'Lone Harp Auto Repair'. I walked through the wide open vehicle door into that sharp oily-rubbery smell you get in garages.

Inside, three or four mechanics were doing mechanic-type things to several cars with the help of Radio One. It looked like a pretty well-equipped workshop, with ramps, inspection pits, and so on. Oil dispensers and other doodahs were built into the walls behind each of the three service bays.

A tall black mechanic strolled towards me, casually swinging a big mole wrench. Close up, I could see that the badge pinned to his brown overalls said, 'Hi, I'm ANGUS – your FOREMAN' – like an Asda checkout girl, for Christ's sake. Aiming a scowl at me, he said:

14

'Guid mornin', surr. How can Ah be of service?'

A bloody West Indian Glaswegian – trying to be nice. I reckon that's about as ferocious as you can get.

'You wouldn't be Quinn by any chance?' I asked. 'I'm supposed to see somebody called Quinn.'

He waved his mole wrench towards a closed door in the far wall.

'In the office,' he said – rude now that he had fulfilled his quota of user-friendly conversation. With a final glare, Angus turned back to the engine block he was operating on.

I knocked and pushed the door open, thinking I would at least get away from the wailing of Radio One – but a new torture jumped out at me. It was mostly twangy guitars, and over it a voice was howling, *'Here's a quarter, call someone who cares'*. As I stepped inside, the noise cut out, and a different voice from behind the desk said:

'Isn't that great Country and Western music?'

I didn't answer, not wanting to start out with an insult. Now that it was quiet, it was just an office. On the big wooden desk I could see a phone, the silenced ghetto-blaster, some files, and the soles of a pair of boots. I looked at them because that was where the voice seemed to come from.

The boots swung aside, revealing a chubby, tanned face furnished with a bushy black moustache though the matching hair showed the beginnings of creeping baldness. Their owner used a lot of even white teeth to grin at me.

'Hello. Would you be Madigan – Kendall Madigan? I'm Patrick Quinn. You can call me Quinn – everybody else does.'

He spoke slowly and stood up to shake hands – about my height, five-eight. I was trying to work out his accent; Irish, I thought, but there was something American about the way he pronounced his words.

We both got seated and Quinn dropped back into his matey act.

'What do you think of my outfit?'

After a moment I realised he wasn't talking about his faded tweed trousers and open-necked shirt. He meant the car repair business.

'Nice.' I thought I might as well hand out a compliment. 'Looks professional.'

15

'Sure it *is* bloody professional. I spent six years in the Buick plant at Fort Worth when I lived over there. The guys here haven't got used to providing a US standard of service yet, but I'm getting them whipped into shape. It's a damn good business – and it's dead straight – completely legitimate.'

'What's that got to do with me?' I asked. 'Are you offering me a job or something?'

I found out later that Quinn hardly ever gave a direct reply. He ignored my question and came at me from a different ball park.

'I know a whole lot about you all, Kenny boy. Clean licence, safe careful driver – no hotshot stuff, competent engineer from way back. You've got the instincts and habits of a pickpocket and you've never been fingered. Am I right so far?'

He had me off balance. I kept my voice in neutral:

'No comment.'

'OK, OK! You have a right to your caution. You don't know me from Daniel O'Connell. Another thing I know is that you don't go around shooting your mouth off; so add discretion into the equation. And you like a laid-back life; so you don't rock the boat as long as things are going well. That means I don't need to fret about stabs in the back from your direction.'

Quinn reached down to the floor and came up with a coffee pot trailing a flex.

'Grab those two mugs off that credenza and help yourself to the fixin's.'

There was a pause while he poured coffee for the two of us and I added milk and sugar.

'OK! Let me fill you in on the deal. I take you on here in a proper regular job . . . all square and legal . . . tax and deductions and all. You get the going rate for a car mechanic but the work is a piece of cake. You collect and deliver customers' cars – all part of Lone Harp's superlative service. Oh, and Angus, my foreman, would be right pleased if you will help out with the stores.'

I was getting confused now – and a bit suspicious. If I wanted a straight job, I would be out looking for one; maybe even try the lawn mower factory. Still, I kept quiet, because Quinn looked as if he had more to say. He went on.

'But you don't get the dog without its fleas. You also work for my other enterprise – in the car-kidnapping industry. It works like this: I get an order for a near-as-dammit-new vehicle, full specification – make, model, colour and all – nothing but upmarket brands. I can also obtain certain information that lets me know exactly where to find a car to match the spec. I let you know where it's located, and you have a couple days to nick the motor. I suppose we can do one every couple of weeks or thereabouts.'

He paused, but went on looking straight at me as if he was trying to pin me to the chair. I kept quiet as long as I could, taking a good look all round the office. Letting it sink in. A couple of grey filing cabinets and a wooden cupboard stood against the walls, three visitor chairs, the usual garage girlie calendars. Another door over to the right of the back wall was closed. Eventually the pressure was too much, and I opened my mouth intending to get rid of the silence. But Quinn was waiting for that and beat me to the draw.

'How do you feel about getting involved in violence?'

I stood up and started towards the door, shaking my head. 'I keep as much distance between me and violence as I can.'

'Come back,' he said quietly. 'That's the *cor*-rect answer. I don't need any hard-ons in the job you'll be doing. I believe in specialisation. If I ever need somebody's head kicked in, I'll use a professional for that job.'

I sat down again.

'All right, I'll admit it sounds interesting,' I said. 'But why should I risk attracting the attention of the law for a straight wage?'

I can't believe I said that; Kenny Madigan the well-known pompous git.

But Quinn gave me a straight answer for once.

'The straight wage is ... like a retainer. You get it for your work at Lone Harp Auto Repair. You also get five hundred pounds every time you bring a nicked car in, that's up front – all in cash. Then when I get paid, you get another five per cent of the pay-off. I believe in taking good care of my business associates.

'You bring the hot cars here at night for Angus to process them. He's the foreman – and he's the only mechanic here who's in on this deal. Another thing, we never steal any of our

17

customers' cars or anything too close to home either. This is an honest-to-God business. OK?'

Quinn leaned forward, confidential like.

'As far as the cops go, you're smart enough to avoid what you called "the attention of the law". The guys I used to be ... associated with in Texas ... they had a saying about the law. It goes *"The Law is an asshole"*.'

It was obvious Quinn thought he had me hooked. He swung round in his swivel chair, aimed his mouth at the closed door behind him. When he shouted, 'Hey, Momma,' he certainly sounded more American than Irish.

We waited. A few moments passed with me wondering what Quinn's mother would look like. Then the door was pulled open from the inside, and I saw a woman standing there. Well, not just a woman; this was a tall, carefully packed blonde; a bimbo, I decided; not in the first flush of youth, but thirty-something, still with her best-before date a few years ahead. Maybe it was the tight Levis and high heels that told me she was a bimbo ... not to mention the Niagara of honey-coloured hair. Definitely not old enough to be Quinn's mother. In fact she was younger than him. She displayed a lot of dental scenery and trilled:

'Hi there, you must be Kenny. It sure is real nice to make your acquaintance.'

She sounded as if she meant it, and there was no doubt about where she came from. We shook hands and she went on:

'I'm real pleased you're gonna join our little enterprise. You can call me Scheri.' She spelled it out.

I started to protest. 'Well, I'm still considering – '

Quinn cut in. 'Nah! It's a done deal. You've already decided. And now you've met the whole family. Momma's the brains around here ... runs the computers and all that kind of shenanigans. She can hack into any network known to man in about ten minutes.' He beamed at her.

Maybe not just a bimbo then. I looked again and persuaded myself I could detect a spark of intelligence behind the baby blues. Among my brain cells, a new bulb lit up.

'Is that how you get your information about cars?'

I could have bit my tongue off. They didn't need to know my guesses about their operation. Too late now, though. Scheri answered.

18

'You sure catch on fast, buddy-boy.'

Quinn headed her off: 'As far as the car-servicing business is concerned, Momma looks after the payroll, the billing, and all the financial stuff, so you would do well to keep on her good side.'

He grinned. 'And she's a real blonde, in case you were wondering.'

He stood up and held out his hand.

'See you on Monday morning; eight thirty on the button.'

I shook his hand. The interview was over.

At the office door, a thought stopped me.

'What about Nick Pearson? Does he work for you?' I asked.

Quinn shook his head.

'He's a small-time villain without the sense of a bucket of frogs. He doesn't know a thing about what we do. Sometimes I use him as a gopher but he's about as much use as Paddy M'Ginty's goat when the chips are down.'

I nodded and left.

'Did you go?'

That was Aileen's first question when she got in from the health food store staggering under a whole week's supply of her seaweed pills and vitamin tablets. I nodded, acting vague and not ready to go into all the details yet. But it was a kind of token resistance; I knew it would not take long for her to milk me dry of every scrap and snippet. Aileen has a black belt in interrogation.

'Right!' she said, catching my nod. 'I've arranged for us to go out for a curry with Sally and this new man of hers. So we better have our board meeting now, before we get changed.'

What Aileen means by a board meeting amounts to making me sit down and discuss all over and round and under a topic till I'm sick of it. It's this mind of hers – it's got a grip like a rottweiler. And she usually steers us into the right decision in the end. I tell her for me it's a very bored meeting, and she could manage just as well without dragging me all round the houses as such. But she always insists that it's vital to our relationship for us to talk everything over before she decides what we should do.

Anyway, calling it a board meeting is not too far off the mark, because our dining-table actually used to be one section of a real boardroom table. I had this great idea about furnishing the maisonette. That was after I saw the kind of money they want for pretty crap furniture in the stores around here.

Well, there's this place in Redditch where they auction off all the contents of the offices from firms that have gone down the grid. And there's loads of really high quality office furniture getting sold for comparative peanuts. So we've got all dead smart stuff at a fraction of the shop prices. Mind you, swivel typing chairs look a bit funny round the dining-table; and I was unfortunately not able to match the colours of the chrome-framed easy chairs with the leather sofa from somebody's reception area. But they're pretty damn smart all the same.

The board meeting went on for about a half-hour before I was grilled to Aileen's satisfaction. That was as long as it took her to pack all her vitamin pills into little daily bags, so it was really neat the way she finished doing both things at exactly the same time. She's dead meticulous about her health food stuff.

Aileen delivered her verdict: 'Right! Part of it's a real job. And the rest sounds less risky than what you've been doing for the last few months. Oh, rats! I think I've got some of the yeast tablets mixed up with the seaweed. Anyway, I think you should go for it; you can always leave if you don't like it.'

So much for shared decision-making. I felt as if I was driving down a motorway with all the exits shut. And what my Auntie Ursula would have called the Four Norsemen of the Apocalypse were breathing up my exhaust pipe.

There would be no more chances to discuss my job for the rest of the evening, thank goodness. Aileen had arranged for us to meet Sally and her new boyfriend in the Cross Keys. Did I mention that Sally looks a bit like Julia Roberts? (But probably not as tall – I don't think Sally would measure forty-four inches from hip to toe.) Well, Aileen's not so bad herself. She was wearing her killer blouse, which makes her look kind of like Sigourney Weaver if you scrunch up your eyes a bit.

The new man was introduced as Neil Cornfoot, and I had to admit, at least at first sight, that he seemed a big improvement over most of Sally's disasters. She usually goes for posh blokes if she can, and her last one one was a public school type – a real chinless wonder. My mate Steve knew him slightly and reckoned he was the sixty-millionth most interesting person in Britain. This Neil looked quite normal. He was actually pretty expensively dressed, in a casual sort of way I couldn't put my finger on – but, you know, definitely a cut above Burton's and River Island.

By the time we moved from the Cross Keys to the Empress of Ranjipoor, we were getting on quite well, having disposed of the weather, and how crowded the town was what with all these Japanese and Italian tourists. Aileen and Sally played the usual women's game of ignoring the menu in favour of swapping trivial pieces of gossip, in the course of which Aileen took it upon herself to announce my new job. That got everybody's attention. I had to give a careful version of how I was going to be a mechanic. Neil sounded quite interested in Lone Harp Auto and its boss. He started asking questions about Quinn that I couldn't answer for one reason or another. I changed the subject.

'So what do you do for a living, Neil?'

Sally answered for him. No wonder she can't keep a man for long.

'Neil's a sergeant in the CID. That's why he's been moved to Stratford – to fill a vacancy here.'

Christ in a bucket – a bloody copper.

The detective sergeant treated us to a sheepish grin. Luckily, the waiter arrived at that moment with his order pad and the preliminary round of lagers. That diverted attention from my open mouth. Thank God I'm not known to the local constabulary. It just goes to show the benefits of being law-abiding as such. I mean, I always pay my road tax and television licence bang on time – and as you know, I'm dead careful about speed limits and everything.

A bit later on, while I started to get to grips with my vindaloo, I asked Neil, 'How do you like this part of the country? It must be quite a change for you.' I thought I'd heard a trace of Newcastle in his accent; not strong though.

He replied, 'Oh no, I'm quite familiar with this area. I got to know it when I was at Warwick University.'

I was a bit surprised.

21

'I didn't know they had coppers stationed at universities. What was that for?'

He shook his head.

'No, I mean when I was an undergraduate – that's where I got my degree.'

Bloody hell!

'You've got a degree? And you joined the police?'

'That's right,' he said. 'They've been recruiting from the universities for years now. Why should the ungodly have all the brains?'

I was quiet for a while, trying to think of any clever coppers I knew. But then I wouldn't, because I carefully avoid rozzers whenever possible. Eventually I got round to trying to make conversation again.

'Well, at least you're off duty tonight. You can relax and forget all that police stuff.'

He looked straight at me and I wished I knew what was going through his mind when he replied, 'Oh, we're never completely off duty, you know. Keep our eyes open all the time.'

He leaned forward and added, 'For instance, there are a couple of shady characters right here in this restaurant – known members of the local criminal fraternity.'

He nodded towards the other side of the restaurant, and I craned my neck to peer round a potted plant, some kind of palm, which was spreading its leaves to the left of my chair. I nearly groaned out loud when I saw Nick Pearson's black head bobbing up and down in conversation with – yes, it must be Nige Prentice. If Nick Pearson saw me, he would be over here like a rat off a hot shovel to ask how I got on with Quinn.

I'll never know how I got through the rest of that meal, shrunk down like an Eskimo's dick behind the potted palm. To make things worse, I was bursting for a pee – lager goes right through me. Before long I was in agony made worse by knowing I couldn't get to the loo without Nick Pearson clocking me.

And my vindaloo was so hot I had to keep dousing myself with more lager. I tried to trick my attention away from my predicament by working out the bill in my head, but my imagination kept coming up with these impossible wild fantasies like: how about if I could smuggle one of these tall empty glasses under the table . . . Or: if only I could get down on my knees and pretend to pray – right in front of that big plant pot ... My imagination isn't very helpful sometimes.

Well, it was an Everest-class emergency, so something had to be done before I either exploded or disgraced myself. Without saying a word to anybody, I picked up the plant pot, palm and all, and staggered to the toilet, carefully keeping these big green leaves between me and Nick Pearson. Happily directing a high-pressure jet at the porcelain, I heaved a huge sigh of relief, and wondered how to explain my sudden love of indoor gardening. Maybe I could say it looked as if it could do with a bit of leaf pruning, and I wanted to make sure in a brighter light ... or – this was better – it needed watering.

Capability Madigan the world-famous plant expert.

My train of thought was interrupted by a familiar voice whining behind me:

''Ere, Kenny, what's the idea? You associating with the filth an' all. Never thought I'd see the day.'

Funny thing! Nobody said a word about me and the palm as such. Not till Aileen got me home, that is.

3

Monday morning at the crack of half-past eight, I was on the doorstep of Lone Harp Auto Repair. There was no sign of Quinn or Scheri, but Angus, the foreman, was expecting me. My first shock came when he issued me with a brown overall with Lone Harp Auto in big letters across the back, and a badge that said, 'Hi, I'm KENNY.' I shouldn't have been surprised, I suppose. I just hadn't thought it through. It's obvious when you think about it; I had to look like just another employee, and this was part of the camouflage.

Angus went on showing me around, without much display of friendliness. We looked at the stores; well organised, I thought. He told me:

'This'll be wan o' yer responsibilities. Keep the stores records; issue parts and supplies tae the mechanics; raise replacement orders; and take deliveries into stock. It's a doddle for an experienced engineer like you. An' it'll allow me tae spend mair time supervising thae dilatory mechanics, and doing the intricate jobs.'

I hadn't bargained for this, but it would be easy enough, so I didn't object. Then, as we were leaving the storeroom, Angus bent down and picked up something I didn't recognise at first. He said:

'An' here's yer velocipede.'

It was one of those folding bicycles that you can put in the boot of a car. It was in its folded state and looked to me as if it might well be rusted solid in that position. Angus enjoyed my puzzlement for a bit, before adding:

'Whit did ye expect – a company car? Ye've got tae fetch and deliver customers' cars, right? So you've nae car to drive for half of every trip. An I'm not aboot tae waste another man's time delivering and fetching you. Ergo, the company bike!'

His very words: *Ergo, the company bike!*

Angus hit me again, when I was down – still staring at Ergo. He thrust a scrap of paper at me saying:

'And here's yer first job. Fetch a Mondeo in from this address. It's at Tiddington – so that'll be a nice salubrious start for ye.'

Kenny Madigan the new challenger in the Tour de France.

While I was struggling to unfold the rotten bike, I happened to look up for a moment. That was the first time I ever saw Angus with a smile on his face.

The whole of my first week was pretty much like that. The work wasn't hard, and it didn't stretch my intellect to breaking point, but it was continuous. Every time I got a job done and started to look forward to taking it easy for a while, Angus would appear like a fairy godmother and give me something else to do.

When there were no cars to pick up or return, he would make sure I was checking stock or tidying up. In fact I started to make some improvements in the way the stores were organised. To be fair, though, I couldn't claim that Angus picked on me specially. He kept all the mechanics hard at it too. I suppose he was just a born organiser.

Still, I did get to know the other three Lone Harp mechanics. They were about the usual kind of mixture you get in any factory or workshop. Jeff was a gossipy middle-aged Brummie. Trevor was about my age and always smelt of Germolene for no obvious reason. Then there was Peasel, only about twenty, who was usually the target for the jokes of the others, on account of he would believe anything he was told. I never did find out why they called him Peasel – it couldn't be his real name.

On the Tuesday Scheri poked her nose out of her den in the back office just long enough to get my details for the payroll and personnel stuff.

During that week Quinn was out a lot of the time, though he did pause once to shake hands with me and say:

'Welcome aboard, Kenny. Sure it's great to have you on the team.'

Quinn's interest in the practical bits of car servicing was enthusiastic but luckily didn't happen too often. He would appear now and again, I suppose when he had a bit of time to spare, and insist on helping one or other of the mechanics. What his help consisted of was usually telling the bloke he was doing it all wrong and how much better these things were done in the General Motors Buick plant in Fort Worth. And maybe he wasn't kidding; once or twice I saw him get so impatient that he shoved the mechanic aside and finished the job in a fraction of the time the manufacturer's manual said it should take.

The guys in the workshop did get a bit annoyed when Quinn interfered, of course, but they had a lot of respect for him. In fact they thought he was wonderful. He really did treat his employees better than these blokes were likely to have been treated by any previous boss. Jeff filled me in on some of it:

'He saw young Peasel all right, did Quinn.'

'What do you mean – saw him all right?'

'Well, it were one morning ... the lad were right miserable and he cocked up a couple o' jobs, like. Turns out he's got a problem on his mind ... his mother's gone and got herself into debt and she's been threatened with the bailiffs coming round.'

Jeff's long face was dead serious and he was talking in a hoarse whisper even though nobody but me was in earshot. He was waiting for encouragement so I supplied it.

'So what happened?'

'We was trying to cover for young Peasel, but it was one of them days when Quinn was crawling all over the workshop ...

he soon cottons on that the lad isn't himself, like. So he yells at him for a while and then orders him into the office. Well, o' course we was all dead certain the poor lad was getting his cards.'

'Well, he's still here so he obviously didn't get fired,' I said. 'Just got a bollocking, I suppose?'

'Well, this is it!' Jeff was reliving the amazement he felt at the time. 'Peasel is in there with Quinn for maybe twenty minutes . . . and then you'll never guess what happens.'

'What happened?' I said, going along with Jeff's sense of drama.

'Well, Peasel comes out all smiles, like it was his birthday . . . Quinn has only given him the money to get his mother out of debt. Would you believe, three hundred quid. Yes, I've got plenty o' time for that man.'

Jeff gave me a nod and got back to work. Angus was heading our way.

So it looked as if Quinn really did take care of his own.

Much of the time when Quinn was in, he stayed in his office and received visitors. Not that there was anything specially eye-catching about them. In fact, in all the time I spent at Lone Harp, the visitors I saw always looked just like normal businessmen or women. Except for Pudding.

I met him on my first day. This stubble-headed character came into the workshop and was making straight for Quinn's office, when he caught sight of me. That caused a detour. He came right up to me and stood there to read my badge of office. He wasn't asking a question when he said:

'Kenny. You're the new driver.'

He was slightly taller than me, but lean all over. Lean face, lean body in a grey T-shirt, lean hairstyle, cold grey eyes, and one ear-ring. No particular accent. I looked straight back at him and asked:

'Who are you?'

'Pudding. You'll get used to seeing me around.'

No smile. No crack in the blank face. He got on with his interrupted journey to Quinn's office.

I did get used to seeing him. Usually he would be escorting a visitor to see Quinn, or maybe a pair of them. While the visitors were having their meeting with Quinn, Pudding would wait outside in the car. Us garage mechanics weren't good enough for him.

Quinn's other callers came in bunches. Not that gangs of them went into his office together. In fact there were never more than two at a time in there. What I mean is that he would spend two or three days having quite a lot of visitors – maybe five or six a day – and then he would be away for a few days.

By the time Friday of that first week came round, I was more than ready for the weekend, what with my legs aching from pedalling Ergo. Aileen just seemed pleased that I had stuck at it, in a (nearly) real job for a whole week. The fact that I hadn't done anything illegal yet, she seemed to take as a kind of bonus.

So it wasn't till my second Monday at Lone Harp Auto that things started to happen. After I'd brought in a couple of cars for MOTs, Quinn called Angus and me into the office and shut off the bloke who was screeching 'Bubba Shot the Juke-box' on his ghetto-blaster.

'All right, Kenny,' he said, 'now you've started to settle in, it's time for you to learn more about this operation. Let's roll.'

He took a bunch of keys from a drawer in his desk, and led the way through to the inner office, where Scheri was steering a computer with one of those mouse things. Quinn ignored her and used one of his keys to open another door on the back wall. We stepped through into a big empty service bay, fully equipped like the ones in the main workshop.

'Angus is in charge of this facility. From outside it looks as if it's not part of Lone Harp's section of the building. The other mechanics know nothing about it, so you don't go shooting your mouth off – right? Show him around, Angus.'

'Aye, well. As you can see, it shares all the services with the other bays through the wall. Except it's also got state o' the art paint-spraying equipment, see.'

Angus pointed it out, and gave me one of his ferocious glares.

'You're not to interfere wi' anything in here, by the way. It's to remain sacrosanct.'

I nodded. There was nothing to be said. Quinn was clumping around the spotless service bay as if he owned it, which I suppose he did. He said:

'You'll be getting your very own key to the big door and you'll have to memorise the code for the security locking system. This is where you bring the hot cars – straight here, no detours.'

A bit unnecessary, that. But I nodded agreement anyway. He added:

'I guess that's all you need to know, Kenny-me-boy. You pinch the car – you drive it here, always at night – you leave the same way you got in – you lock up, and bugger off home. And you don't remember a damn thing. Right? Oh, an' the door to the office is kept locked tight; so you can forget any ideas about snooping around.'

As if I would! I wondered if Angus had a key to the office door. But what did I care? The less my involvement, the better. Still, I couldn't resist a question. Me and my big mouth.

'What if somebody rents the unused part of the building? They might see enough to get suspicious.'

Quinn grinned at me with most of his teeth.

'Don't you worry your head about that, my lad. I can guarantee there won't be anybody getting suspicious in there. It's already rented – by me. And you better keep your nose out of there as well.'

I got my first assignment the very next day. Quinn called me into the office. Scheri was sitting demurely by his side, holding a bunch of papers and looking about as businesslike as anybody could in a blouse as well-filled as hers was. Quinn took charge:

'Are you feeling bright-eyed and bushy-tailed, Kenny? You better be, because this is where you start making a positive contribution to our little enterprise. Show him his target, Momma.'

Scheri slid a sheet of paper across the desk for me to pick up. It had a neatly printed description of a car. A silver Lexus 400 – at least fifty thousand quid's worth of motor. The description didn't end there, it included the registration number; engine size and type – 4 litre V8; the VIN (Vehicle Identification Number); date of registration – Christ, it was less than a month old; a detailed specification followed. Below that was a name – David Rodgers – and an address in Evesham. His business address was there too – also in Evesham.

'I need it parked in the secret bay by Thursday night – latest,' Quinn said.

I started to fold the paper, so I could tuck it away somewhere safe, but Scheri stopped me.

'No, honey. You don't get to keep that. Just memorise the address and enough data so you can recognise the automobile.'

I did as I was told, then handed back the paper. Quinn picked up a lighter from the desk, and used it to set fire to one corner of the sheet. Once it was fully alight, he dropped it into the metal waste bin. He turned back to me.

'You make your own arrangements. I don't give a shit how you do it – just don't screw up. When you bring it in, you'll get the first instalment of your cut. It'll be in a brown envelope on the bench in there.'

He jerked his head in the direction of 'in there'. I got the feeling that Quinn didn't like referring to the 'secret bay' and I thought of suggesting it should be called Moonlight Bay. But Quinn had his serious expression switched on, so I scraped together enough sense to keep my mouth shut.

'Good luck, honey.' That was Scheri. She added, 'I'm sure you'll come through for us.'

Quinn looked at his watch and then looked at me.

'OK, Kenny. I guess that's about it. Best of luck. And now if you don't mind, I'm expecting company.'

Nobody has ever accused me of not being able to take a hint. I got out.

But I couldn't help keeping an eye open from the workshop to see what Quinn's 'company' would look like. About ten minutes later, while I was chatting with Jeff, Pudding came through directing the visitor over to the office. Just another businessman, dressed in the usual suit and stuff. Boring but very expensive-looking. Nobody I had ever seen before.

'Now what the bloody hell would he be doing here?'

That was Jeff, sounding surprised.

'You know that bloke?' I asked him.

'Well, not *know* him – not exactly. I don't like ... *know* him, but I know who he is all right. My lad Horace does casual work for him ... odd jobs and the like in his garden. Great big house he's got, near Solihull.'

'Yeah,' I said, 'he looks to be that sort of bloke. He's definitely not one of our customers, as such. But what kind of business is he in, do you think?'

'Ooh,' Jeff said in that whiney way Brummies sometimes do, 'no mystery about that, to be sure. That's Mr Summerbee. He owns a big shop right in the centre of Birmingham.'

It occurred to me that Mr Summerbee didn't look like a happy businessman; but we've all got our troubles, I suppose.

The way I approached that first car-nicking operation for Quinn was a model for all the jobs that came after. The first thing was to get familiar with the area in daylight without looking suspicious. After I did my morning pick-ups, I mentioned to Angus that I had a job to do for Quinn. He obviously knew already.

'Aye, don't worry aboot getting back here in time to return this lot. We'll handle it.'

He straightened up and left Trevor to get on with a gearbox job on his own.

'We'll see you in the morning then.' He grinned and added, 'Best of British – and be circumspect.'

That was a turn-up. Even Angus was being friendly now. I felt like flavour of the month.

I put Ergo in the boot of my own five-year-old Cavalier and drove the fifteen miles to Evesham. I left the Cavalier in a pay-and-display and rode off to find the scene of my first criminal act – in this job anyhow. It occurred to me that I could still have pulled out.

I wish to God I had.

Biking slowly around the target area in my old jeans and pullover, I fancied I looked like a gardener or a bloke who does odd jobs for the well-heeled. The house where the Lexus lived had 'in' and 'out' drives – tarmac, fortunately; gravel can be pretty noisy. No sign of the motor itself – just a smart white Toyota in front of the big double garage, which was shut. Must be the wife's.

OK, now I looked for the most direct route to the bypass. As I think I've already said, preparation is dead essential in this game. I knew a bloke once who nicked a car in a residential area, and had to make three-point turns in four cul-de-sacs before he found the main road. But *he* was a thicko.

30

I had decided I would call off the job if there was the least sign of it going pear-shaped, like if I was spotted by a neighbour in some way that they were likely to remember and connect me with the later disappearance of a car. So my heart sank when I was hailed by a woman about half a dozen houses away from the Lexus place. She must have been about fifty, and she was prodding at a bush in her front garden in a blue frock and high heels.

'I say, fellow,' she called. I stopped and stood astride the bike. 'Have you finished doing Mrs Baxter's yet?'

'Aar . . .' I answered. That could mean anything – and that's how they talk in Evesham.

'Right,' she said, 'I've got a nice little job for you. I want mine pollarded the minute you're free. I'll leave the shed unlocked, and you can get started first thing in the morning. The thrushes have left the nest now, so there's no need to delay any longer.' She didn't say 'my good man' but she looked it.

'Aar . . .' I said again, though it hadn't worked before. Thinking fast, I added, 'Sorry, missus, I promised to prune ole Mrs Ramage's oleanders. I'll get back to you when it's done.' As I said it, I was wondering what the hell an oleander is. Then without giving her a chance to say any more, I started pedalling as fast as I could, with her angry stare burning a hole in the back of my neck. Oh, well. No harm done. At least she didn't think I was a suspicious character.

The return of Capability Madigan, world-famous gardening expert.

The next thing was to take a look at the business address. Not that I thought for a minute of nicking the car from there – but it's a good idea to find out as much as you can about your target's present owner, not to mention his habits. Anyway, I hadn't eyeballed the motor yet, as Quinn would likely have put it. And there it was, all sleek and shiny, parked outside a building with a brass plate telling the world 'David Rodgers Associates'.

Looks as if associating brings in a lot of money.

That was all I needed. I went back to the house later on in the evening to see what kind of overnight arrangements they had for the car. You'd be amazed how many people have their garage so cluttered with junk that there's no room for cars. This one was all right though; I was lucky enough to see the Lexus being reversed into the garage for the night, and the automatic double door closing in front of it.

Now you might think that would make my job harder, but you'd be dead wrong. If a car is outside, I'm exposed to the eyes of the whole world for the two minutes or so that it might take me to unlock it and get the engine started. But who ever locks a car when it's sitting in their own garage? People are dead careless. Fortunately.

I was willing to bet that the person-sized door in the back of this garage wouldn't be locked. Not that there would be much of a problem if it was. At least, not for a person with my skills.

Thanks to my preparation, it was a breeze. I managed to talk Aileen into dropping me in Evesham town centre late on the Thursday night (she complained about this, and said she would never do it again). By the time I got to the target on foot, it was after midnight, and the house was in darkness.

The back door of the garage was unlocked, and, would you believe it, the keys were in the ignition of the Lexus. I checked around the instruments and stuff by the internal light. The engine started at the first touch and ran practically in silence. Then I pressed the button on the remote control for the garage door – I had found it clipped to the sun visor – and eased the big car out into the night. A hundred yards down the road, I switched the lights on, and made for Stratford, keeping to country roads as much as I could, just in case.

Kenny Madigan, carnapper to the crowned heads of Europe.

My first real job for Quinn was done – except for one small detail, and that was really for my peace of mind. When I got back home, I wrote down all the details I had memorised, on one of these little yellow note things – you know, the ones with the sticky strip on the back. Then I looked for a book that nobody would ever want to read. That was easy.

Last year, Aileen got hooked into buying these condensed books from Reader's Digest in the hope of winning their grand draw. She accumulated nearly a dozen before she managed to stop them coming. Aileen thought they looked smart in the glass-fronted cabinet, though as I think I've mentioned before, she really wanted me to put up a proper bookshelf. Anyway, I stuck the car details to a page somewhere in the middle of *The Mill on the Floss*. It was written by Silas Marner, I think. Later on, the dirt on all the other cars went into the same book. You never know when you're going to need some insurance.

At Lone Harp the next morning, Quinn was in a good mood. He called me into the office.

'Nice job, Kenny,' he told me. 'Sure and it was a good day when I hired you.'

His brows and moustache went up together as his teeth joined in the smile that was already lighting his eyes. It looked to me like genuine pleasure. He added:

'You'll be joining me an' the boys tonight in the Queen's Head?'

'Why, what's on?' I asked, though I had heard something about it from the mechanics.

'Oh, it's just a little thing we do every now and then. I take all the guys out for a night on the town. The drinks are on me, an' we have ourselves a ball. It's great for morale as well. How's about it?'

'OK, why not?' I said.

I got to the Queen's Head about eight. They were at a table in the far corner – Quinn and the three mechanics and Angus. No sign of Pudding or Scheri. Quinn looked to be in his element, surrounded by his fans. He waved me over and everybody shuffled around to make room. A pint of bitter appeared in front of me as if by magic. Apparently Quinn had left enough money with the barman to keep us drinking for about a week, so we were getting service like nobody had ever seen before in that pub.

Quinn was the centre of attraction of course, and enjoying himself hugely. He was entertaining the blokes with stories about his experiences in Texas. When I arrived he was telling about the effect America had on him when he first went there as an innocent farm lad from Donegal. Apparently Country and Western music is really big in Ireland, so he really flipped on finding himself living in the place the stuff comes from. I refrained from saying it should have stayed there. But Quinn was such an engaging character, that night at least, that along with everyone else, I couldn't help liking him.

Having worked in a factory myself, I could appreciate his tales about the crazy things that went on in the Buick plant at Fort Worth. One of them was about the time the company president – the boss of the whole of General Motors, that is – was coming to inspect the plant. Well, it was like a visit from God, though this president's name was something ordinary – Roger Smith, I think. So the whole place was painted and tarted up for the occasion. Trouble was, there had been an almighty cock-up (Quinn called it a 'snafu') by Production Control which resulted in a whole year's supply of fuel tanks being delivered all at once. These fuel tanks were blocking corridors all over the plant because there wasn't enough room for them all in the stores. So what they did was, they hired a fleet of trucks, loaded them up with the fuel tanks and had them driven around Fort Worth all day while the company president and his 'posse of vice-presidents' admired how nice and efficient the factory looked.

Quinn had the knack of telling a story. He spun that one out and had us curling up in laughter with his impression of the Yankee plant manager banging his head on his desk and groaning, 'Why couldn't they have been cigar lighters?'

I was quite pleased to hear that the biggest company in the world is just as subject to Murphy's Law as all its smaller brothers.

Later on, around my fourth pint, we somehow got around to talking about snooker and comparing it with pool, the nearest equivalent they have in America. Quinn had never played snooker while he was growing up in Ireland, but he claimed to have become a 'real mean pool player' in America. In fact he said he used to win money 'hustling pool', while Trevor claimed to be some kind of hotshot snooker player.

'It's all the same kinda skills in both games,' Quinn said to Trevor. 'I bet you twenty quid I could beat your ass off at snooker even though I never played the game before.'

This was a great chance for me to keep my mouth firmly shut. But of course I didn't.

'Why don't we go up to the snooker club and find out?' I said. 'I'm a member there so I can sign you in. And they have a bar, so we can keep drinking.'

So off we all went. All except Angus, that is – he must have slipped away when nobody was looking.

I should have realised what would happen. Quinn was pretty good – you could see that. But the proportions of the table were different from what he was used to, and that meant that all the angles were different. He never had a chance against Trevor, who hadn't lied about his ability.

At first, Quinn was dead confident, all matey and full of wisecracks. But as Trevor forged ahead, he got dead quiet. Quinn's face was starting to match the red balls, and I could see a vein throbbing in his neck when he leaned over his cue to take aim.

Finally it was too much. He snapped the cue over his knee, threw the pieces on the table, added three twenty-pound notes, and walked out without a word. I wouldn't have cared to be in Quinn's way just then.

4

As I said before, that first car operation set the pattern. I don't mean the way I did the actual nicking; that varied a lot depending on circumstances. And don't get the idea that they were all as easy as that first one. In fact all my skills were needed at one time or another. What I mean about the same pattern is my general approach of getting to know the terrain over two or three days, and planning the job carefully.

The second one came two weeks later.

And it went on like that. Sometimes there would be one every week for a while; and occasionally a couple of weeks would pass without me having to exercise my car-nicking skills. Usually it was as easy as that first one. It's amazing how people have regular habits. Quite often I'd find that a target car's owner would regularly work late at the office, which was fine for me so long as the car was parked out of sight of the office windows. Or he (sometimes she) would drop in for a quiet pint or a few gin and tonics at a particular pub on the way home every night.

And I kept up my insurance premiums; Aileen's condensed books acquired quite a collection of yellow notelets. All stuck to pages, too – no chance of them falling out if the book was shaken by the spine.

One thing I had to change though. That was my arrangement for getting myself to the cars for the actual nicking, as such, seeing as they were always a good distance away from Stratford. Aileen was definitely a non-starter; she made that dead clear. My first idea was to nick any old car in Stratford, and dump it an easy walk away from the target – but that was doubling the risk for no good reason. I put the problem to Quinn, and suggested that maybe Angus could deliver me. Well, I thought I better get my idea in first in case Quinn assigned Pudding to the job. That bloke would give Dracula the creeps. Anyway, Angus it was.

The second car I nicked was as hard as they get. This BMW was parked on the street at night – in Warwick – and the owner wasn't considerate enough to leave it unlocked.

Well, at least it's in a quiet street, but you can imagine how exposed I feel working at the door lock with my set of fine wire picks. It only takes a couple of minutes, but feels like hours. Then I'm safe inside working at the screws of the cowling over the steering column by the light of my little torch. Once I get that off, it's easy to bypass the ignition switch with my own trusty piece of wire which has crocodile clips on both ends. Designed for the purpose, you might say.

Then another bit of dangerous exposure. I pull the bonnet release lever and hop out to operate the starter motor. That takes another essential piece of my equipment; a length of heavy cable, well insulated. When I hold one end of this cable against the terminal on the starter motor and touch the other end to the positive terminal of the battery, the starter motor turns. Obviously. I hold it there till the engine catches, which is almost immediate this time, luckily. Then I'm back inside. Just one more obstacle; the steering lock. But I have a key that frees up ninety per cent of steering locks. You can buy these keys by mail order, by the way. This particular one is a member of the ninety per cent – saves me taking another ten seconds to force the unit. Now I can drive away. The whole thing has taken me almost ten minutes of concentration.

Now I can start to sweat and worry about what might have happened if some sleepless punter had looked out of a window and called the police.

Actually that business with the starter motor and battery is pretty crude. If you know the model of car well enough, or study the workshop manual, you can operate the starter from the bundle of spaghetti around the ignition switch without having to get under the bonnet. But this was a new model of BMW, and Lone Harp didn't have a manual for it.

I got to know Angus quite well through him driving me to the scenes, and we gradually became friends, kind of. He was a good bloke when you got to know him. A bit strange sometimes, though. Apart from dropping me within striking distance of the target, he wanted to know nothing about what he called the 'provenance' of the motors whose identity he changed.

As I got more friendly with Angus, I tried in a roundabout way to get him to tell me what he knew about Quinn and Scheri. He thought they were probably married, but wasn't sure: he did know that they lived together but not where. On one journey, I think it was to somewhere up beyond Studley, I brought up another subject I couldn't help feeling curious about. I was sure it must have something to do with the stolen car racket.

'Do you know what Quinn uses the other part of our building for? I've never seen anybody going in there – it just seems to stay locked up all the time.'

'Aye,' he said, 'so it does – in the daytime. But sometimes when I'm working on the stolen cars at night, I can hear the noise of work going on in there.'

That really took me by surprise. I asked:

'Then it's got nothing to do with the motors? I mean, you would know wouldn't you – you're in charge of the nicked cars while they're there.'

'I suppose I would find out. But don't forget – I just know my wee bit. I change a car's identity – Quinn supplies the new numbers and tells me what colour to paint it. A couple of days later Quinn lets me know what time it's being picked up – it's always at night – and I come in to hand it over to this bloke – he talks like a Londoner. He gets dropped outside, in the street; I open the door, and he drives the car away.'

'So they don't get stored in the unused section?'

'No. But one night when I was outside having a breath of fresh air away from the paint fumes, a truck came round the back of the building and that big door was opened from the inside. The truck drove straight in and the doors were shut in a flash. I don't think I want to know what goes on in there, but I have heard that Quinn's got an interest in an antique furniture business. It might be something to do wi' that.'

Angus took his eyes off the road for a moment to give me a serious look:

'And if you've got the brains of a tattie bogle, you'll keep yer own counsel. Yon Quinn is a fucking dangerous man to anybody that causes trouble – or knows too much. And that zombie they call Pudding – if he ever comes near me, he'll get his heid in his hands to play with. A right malignant bastard if ever I saw one.'

'Still,' I said, 'Quinn's a bloody good boss to work for, isn't he? Looks after his workers really well, doesn't he?'

'Oh, ye've heard aboot him giving the money tae Peasel, then? Aye, that was an excellent thing to do on the face of it. Call me cynical, but Quinn might think it was a reasonable price to pay for a bunch of devoted fans. Look at the control he's got over the mechanics now.'

Angus was still a mystery to me at this time. He was a quiet man, who never gave out any information about his private life. For a while I thought he might be gay, because he didn't join in the banter of the mechanics. They were always going on about the great tits on this month's chick on the garage calendar ... what they would like to do to that Sharon Stone. That kind of macho rubbish.

However, to get back to Angus, I decided he probably wasn't gay because he seemed a lot more masculine – you know, more of a real man – than that shower in the workshop. Maybe it was just being black among all us white people that made him act with more dignity.

I suppose Angus must have started to trust me after a while, because one night when he was lined up to give me a lift, he took me to his house. It was a neat semi on one of those newish estates off to the left going up Birmingham Road.

'Come away in an' we'll have some coffee' he said. 'You don't want to be too early, in your kind of enterprise.'

I thought, Christ, I hope he's not going to make a pass at me, remembering my suspicion about Angus perhaps being gay. But I went in and took a seat in the living-room. His eyes swept around as if he was looking at the place for the first time.

'It's mebbe a wee bit spartan, but I canny be doing with a lot of ornaments and bric-à-brac.'

It looked all right to me; dead neat and everything. He was right about the lack of ornaments – unless models counted as ornaments. There must have been dozens of them, on shelves, a table, and even a couple of big ones on the carpet. I spotted the Eiffel Tower, Tower Bridge, the Leaning Tower of Pisa, and that one that used to be the Post Office Tower but is now the BT Tower, I suppose. Angus followed my glance.

'Aye, man, that's my hobby. They're all made out of match-sticks, by the way. I got a bit obsessed with towers for a while, but I've managed tae break that habit. This one I'm working on now is the Sydney Opera House – it's gonny be my *tour de force*.'

I was saved from having to think of something to say by a new arrival on the scene. At first I thought she was a young girl about fourteen years old, but a look at her face under the light told me she must be nearly thirty. I had been misled by the fact that she was only five foot one and very slim. Her red hair was cut short and was curly all over. She was carrying a tray.

'Here's your coffee and a wee biscuit,' she said, smiling at me. Another Glaswegian.

Angus beamed as if this woman was the light of his life.

'Meet my wife, Senga,' he said proudly.

While we drank our coffee, I was treated to a display of domestic bliss. These two were obviously crazy about each other. So much so that I began to feel as if I was intruding on their private world.

After that first visit, we changed our routine. When I was going to nick a car, Angus and I would work late at Lone Harp and then go straight from work to his house. In warm weather, Angus didn't drive to work. He liked to walk, taking a short cut through some back alleys. It was a great summer – weatherwise at least. We were usually on foot when we went to his place where we would always have coffee and biscuits with Senga. She turned out to be a really nice person. And of course I got to see the gradual development of the Sydney Opera House.

After a few successful operations, I had the idea of leaving my own car parked in a quiet place beforehand so that it would be convenient to make a short stop beside it with the hot car. I was pretty sure that neither Quinn nor the future owners of the stolen cars would be interested in any bits and pieces they might contain. But I was.

There was no need for Quinn to know. I was careful enough to use different places; one or other of the big supermarket car-parks, or a pay-and-display that was free after six o'clock – and fairly empty. Not that I ever got anything very valuable, except once. Cellular phones were fairly common, though; and I could get rid of them easy enough through Ernie Hodges the fence in Leamington. Ernie paid out a small fraction of what they were worth, and his brother-in-law sold them from a market stall at car boot sales all round the area.

Still, it was quick money, and though I didn't really need it, I just couldn't resist the opportunity.

That one valuable thing I mentioned was a necklace with sparkly stones in different colours, that I found in a Jaguar. I don't know much about jewellery, but it looked good to me. I thought about keeping it for Aileen, but that's a mug's game if the article is valuable. Ernie the fence took a close look, and said he wouldn't touch it with a tyre lever. However, he said he thought he might be able to get rid of it for me 'through the trade'. I shrugged and left it with him, not expecting to hear any more about it. So I was pretty surprised a couple of weeks later when Ernie handed me an envelope containing three hundred quid.

Christ, that necklace must have been worth quite a few thousand for me to get that much after Ernie and God knows who else took their cut.

I remember that Jag very well for another reason. For one thing, it was the easiest job I ever did for Quinn. It was in a village over towards Worcester, quite a distance away. I spent a couple of days casing the whole area with my usual attention to detail, and it was pretty typical – quiet, classy area, well-dressed wife, two kids, big house with a separate double garage off to the side.

During the two days I had been watching, the car was locked away in the garage each night. But when I finally turned up, courtesy of Angus, to make the pick-up, that's what it turned out to be – a straight pick-up. House in darkness, no sign of anybody for miles, Jag not even in the garage – just sitting there inside the open gate, facing the street. I could hardly believe my luck when I found the driver's door unlocked and the key in the ignition, all ready to go. It's nothing less than criminal how careless some people can be.

There was nothing remarkable about the car itself, except of course for the item of jewellery I mentioned. The necklace was in a brown envelope on the dashboard which also contained a piece of paper with 'You have been warned' printed on it in red marker. Kids larking about with Mummy's valuables, I suppose. I dumped the paper and envelope in a litter bin at the supermarket.

The other reason I remember that Jag was that when I got it back to Lone Harp Auto, there was a reception committee. Quinn and Pudding were waiting for me in the secret bay looking anxious.

'Has anybody been following you?'

That was Quinn's first question.

'No chance,' I said, feeling a bit insulted. Being in the line of work that I'm in, one thing I'm always aware of is what other traffic is on the road, especially behind me.

Quinn ordered me out of the car and there was no more conversation. He just made me wait while the two of them carried out a thorough search of the motor. And I don't mean a superficial turnover like I do in Tesco's car-park. They had the spare wheel out, they searched the engine compartment, they even had the door panels off and the back seat out.

When they had finished, and apparently not found whatever they were looking for, Quinn relaxed a bit.

'OK, buddy,' he said to Pudding, 'you might as well knock off now. See you when you get back from Manchester.'

Pudding never said a word; just opened the door enough to get his pale face through, and left. Quinn turned to me.

'It's OK, Kenny. I'm not putting you down. Only I got word that we might have been set up. The order I got was so damned specific that it could only have led us to this very motor. I did some checking up tonight, and you know what?'

I shook my head.

'Well ... let's just say the order came from a different source – not through my usual contacts. They knew the right buttons to press though. Maybe it's nothing at all to worry about.'

He still looked worried to me. It was the first time I ever saw Quinn concerned about anything. My money was on the bench as usual. I picked it up and went home.

Maybe that 'You have been warned' was more than just a kid's game. But I somehow felt that Quinn had got the message even without the note.

Later, I brought the subject up with Angus.

'What happened to that last car I brought in – the Jaguar?' I asked him.

'Funny you should ask aboot that,' he replied. 'Quinn would-nae let me touch it; wouldnae even let me go to the store to get the paint that we ordered for the job, or change the plates or anything. The usual bloke collected it just the way it was.'

'Why would Quinn do that, do you think?'

Angus shrugged.

'What do I care? I still got paid as much as if I had given it the full works.'

5

Then there was Scheri; another mysterious person. Where did she fit into the set-up? Could she be the brains behind the whole thing? Or was she just playing the bimbo part alongside Quinn? I never really found out anything about her, as such, till I'd been working at Lone Harp for about a month.

The mechanics were always going on about her – among themselves, like, and sniggering quite a lot. Well, they would do, wouldn't they? They hadn't ever seen a chick – I mean a woman – like her before.

This particular day I had a question about my tax code. Well, it would be more true to say that Aileen wanted more information about my tax code. So anyway, I was hanging around in the workshop, listening to the mechanics' crude chat, and watching for Scheri to turn up so I could ask about the tax thing.

Eventually, her red Honda appeared outside, and she swayed into the shop heading for the office, just as Trevor, the Germolene Kid, was yelling something to Peasel . . . something like:

'What would you do with a five-foot-ten Barbie doll in a thunderstorm?'

Another crack about Scheri. She must have heard it. I gave her time to get settled in her office; you know, get the computers switched on, and water boiled for the coffee. Then I went in, through the first office (Quinn was out). I knocked on the inner door and heard 'Come on in,' so I went on in.

'Hi there, Kenny,' she said brightly, flashing one of her high-octane smiles. 'Set yourself down and drink some coffee with me.'

'Thanks, Scheri. I'm sorry about the remarks you heard from the blokes out there.' For some reason I felt responsible for the ignorance of my fellow countrymen. I blundered on, 'I hope you don't think you'll get sexual harassment from everybody in England.'

Scheri laughed and poured coffee into a mug for me. Her laugh was a more pleasant sound than I would have expected.

'Harassment, you call that harassment?'

She pronounced it har*a*ssment, with the stress on the second syllable.

'Well, thanks for your concern, Kenny. But where I come from, the local rednecks think harass is two words.'

Good one, that. I tucked it away in my mind for telling to my mate Steve; he would appreciate it.

'Where *do* you come from?' I asked her. 'I was wondering about that.'

'Waxahachie,' she said, as if I should know where that is. Seeing my blank look, she added, 'Waxahachie, Texas . . . it's a small city, just about big enough to have a set of traffic lights on Main Street ... but I high-tailed it outa there, soon as I graduated out of high school. Went to Dallas and worked as a dancer in a topless honky-tonk to pay my way through college. So I reckon I can handle any shit *these* hicks want to throw at me.'

I avoided the topless thing. I could imagine she would be a big attraction.

'College? Do you mean, like university? Have you got a degree, then?'

'Yup ... Computer Science.'

Christ! I'm surrounded by intellectuals. How could I ever have thought of this woman as a recycled bimbo ... or that she was in need of my protection?

I looked around for a way to change the subject, and my eye snagged on the computer equipment lined up on the tables against the long wall of the office. There were two screens lit up. One of them had a jumble of words and numbers that meant nothing to me; but the other one showed a list of furniture with lines saying things like 'Edwardian walnut escritoire', and 'Victorian dining-table'. I nodded towards this screen and said, 'Is that an inventory of your furniture? Maybe I can help if you're trying to fix up insurance. My mate Steve is in the insurance business.'

I can never resist trying to help an attractive woman. Except when Aileen's around, of course.

'Nah,' Scheri replied. 'Quinn and me, we rent a place in Snitterfield. It's furnished and the insurance is all bundled in with the rent. But thanks, anyway. What you see on the screen is a list of the furniture that came in on the last shipment.'

'What do you mean "came in" – into where?'

'Into the back part of the building, of course,' she said. 'That's where Quinn stores the antiques till they're ready to ship out.'

'Oh,' I said, deciding not to chase that rabbit any more, and thinking Angus was dead right not to know too much about Quinn's shady deals. I swallowed some coffee and changed the subject:

'It's really you that runs this place, as such, isn't it? I mean, you handle all the paperwork and accounts, worksheets, payroll, invoicing, ordering, and all these kind of things. Angus checks the customers' cars in and out and supervises the work, and I look after the stores. So what does Quinn do?'

'Well, Quinn's the head honcho, and I guess you could say that he bankrolls the operation. Anyhow, he's got his fingers in plenty of other pies, so he's pretty goddam busy one way and another, even when he's someplace else. He's got contacts everyplace.'

'Right,' I said, wondering about those other pies and thinking that antique furniture was a pretty funny kind of pie for a car-laundering garage owner to have a finger in. But I felt I'd already been nosy enough. Besides, what did I care? I reminded myself that the less I knew about Quinn, the better. Probably.

When I finished my coffee, Scheri came over to pick up my mug, and I could feel the heat of her body as she leaned over me maybe a bit closer than she needed to. She smiled and said:

'Don't forget you can come in and have coffee with me any old time you like, Kenny. I don't often get anybody civilised to chew the fat with.'

She winked at me then, and it made me feel that I had brought some sunshine into her life. I left the office and went back to the storeroom, clean forgetting my tax code query. Luckily, Aileen forgot all about it as well.

Speaking of Aileen, I suppose I should put the record straight and mention that we're not actually married. Well, we talked about getting hitched, around the time we started living together. About two years ago, that was. I was quite willing, but Aileen said no, let's wait and see if you grow up and I said what did she mean by that and she said never mind she was only joking. Which I thought was a bit strange because Aileen hasn't got much of a sense of humour. Not like me.

Just once in all this time, the smooth carnapping system failed. Angus dropped me off in Winchcombe on what looked like a routine job. When I got inside the garage – no black Mercedes. Well, I can't prevent people going away for a few days just so I can nick their car. Anyway there I was, stuck twenty miles from home without transport. I managed to hitch a lift back to Stratford, thanks to a Safeway delivery driver taking pity on me.

I expected Quinn to throw a tantrum, but he just shrugged and muttered something about 'can't help having a bit of a cock-up now and again – just forget it'. It seemed that he had completely lost interest in that Merc, because he didn't even want me to go back and try again.

It was not until the day after that it suddenly struck me I could have got home dead easy just by nicking a car – any car. It just goes to show how basically honest I am.

On the whole, that was a pretty good time for me; that six months or so. I admitted as much to my mate Steve over a couple of pints in the Bell. Steve and I have been pretty close friends since about the age of seven, but we don't get together so much these days – not since he married that Sheila and saddled himself with a dirty great mortgage. For some reason Sheila thinks I'm a bad influence on Steve, so our long nights at the snooker club and trips to Villa's home matches are things of the past. Even our get-togethers in the pub have been getting further apart. Another thing is that I don't think Steve likes Aileen very much. He's never actually said so, as such; though he once described her as 'a bit waspish', whatever that means.

Steve has never done anything dodgy in his life; unless you count working in the head office of a big insurance company, where he's steadily moving up the management tree. Still, he's always interested to hear about what I've been getting up to. He was fascinated by the Quinn organisation, so I ended up telling him everything I knew about it. Naturally the business about the computers caught his attention.

Steve is pretty familiar with computers; not to the extent of writing programs, I don't think; but he uses a computer all the time at work, and he's got one he plays around with at home.

It occurred to me to ask him what he thought about all the car information Scheri was getting hold of.

'Do you think she's . . . what do you call it . . . hacking into the DVLC computer in Swansea?' I asked.

Steve scratched his head and looked gormless like he always does when he's considering something.

'No, I don't think so,' he said, 'the DVLC computers will have really tight security. Anyway, they don't keep a whole lot of information about cars at the DVLC. They're only concerned about linking the registration with an owner, and collecting the tax.'

He gave me a funny look and added, 'But you know that perfectly well, Kenny. There isn't much you don't know about cars.'

Of course I knew that. I was only trying to prod him to come up with a better answer. I said:

'All right then, Smartarse, how does she do it then?'

'Well, my guess is she's hacking into the dealer networks. You see, every car dealer is hooked into a network controlled by the car maker whose motors they flog. And they keep every possible detail about every car they sell, and the punter they sold it to. Car dealers don't usually give a damn about security and passwords and such, so they'd be easy meat for an expert hacker.'

I nodded. That sounded pretty reasonable.

Like I said, it was a good time for me. Aileen really appreciated the money I was bringing home. She said it gave her a chance to dress as well as Sally; and of course we had to go out a lot more in the extra evenings that I now had to spare. We quite often made up a foursome with Sally and Neil. Amazing, that – it was starting to look as if Sally had learned how to keep a man at last. And Neil turned out to be a pretty decent bloke, too – considering he's a copper, anyway.

It was through going out with Sally and Neil that I saw something else I wasn't supposed to see. Aileen and I had arranged to meet them in the Cross Keys one evening, but when we got there, Neil was by himself. Sally had phoned to say she had to work late. See, Sally works in an office in Knowle which is a good fifteen miles north of Stratford. She drives there in her little Fiesta.

Anyway, Sally had suggested that we should go up to Knowle to meet her and we could go to this great pub that had a proper restaurant attached. Being Sally, and dead bossy as she is, she had gone right ahead and booked a table for us there. How's that for putting on airs – a pub where you need to have a reservation! So off the three of us went in my car, so that Neil could come back with Sally.

Well, we got there and I have to admit it really was quite smart – dead pretentious though, with French names for the dishes on the menu. Still, they had enough sense to put a description in English beside each one. It was the kind of place where they don't allow you to get to your table until you've bought expensive drinks at the bar while drooling over the menu. When we finally reached our table I had a good look round while trying to ignore Aileen and Sally who were going on about how nice the flowers were.

I spotted a face I had seen before – Summerbee the shopkeeper, who visited Quinn that time. He was at a table for two with a woman. Well, Jeff the Brummie said he lived in Solihull so this place would be quite local for him. A prosperous businessman having a quiet dinner with his wife.

I was just sawing into my '8 oz tender sirloin steak chargrilled to my taste with a creamy peppercorn sauce and a selection of today's most succulent vegetables', when something happened that made me go cold inside – and nearly put the mockers on my appetite. He looked out of place there, in his faded grey T-shirt, pale face and stubbly haircut.

Pudding. I thought at first that he was coming for me but I don't think he even saw me. His eyes were fixed somewhere else and never blinked once as he bee-lined towards Summerbee.

Pudding tapped the businessman on the shoulder and suddenly they were both as white-faced as each other. Nothing was said. Pudding jerked his head in a 'follow me' way, and walked towards the exit. Mr Summerbee followed. He didn't come back to finish his sole véronique. After a while a waiter came and said something to the woman, who got up and left looking very agitated. Nobody else in the resaurant seemed to notice anything – not even our very own supercop. I was confused. I didn't even know if I was glad that Neil had missed the whole thing because of facing the wrong way.

I nipped out to the loo in the lull before the dessert trolley. Out of sight of our table I waylaid the waiter and asked him about that customer who seemed to have been taken ill.

'Well, he's not ill, exactly,' he told me. 'The gentleman went out to his car – to fetch something, I suppose – and got mugged in the car-park. He's been taken away in an ambulance.'

'Christ!' I said. 'How bad is he?'

The waiter shrugged.

'Dunno, mate. But he was unconscious. Looked pretty bloody nasty to me.'

We both agreed that nobody is safe anywhere any more. And we didn't know what the world was coming to. I made my way back to our table feeling almost as pale as Pudding, and stayed pretty quiet for the rest of the evening.

I never heard anything more about that incident. Some time later it occurred to me to ask Jeff how his son was doing. Was he still working at that posh house in Solihull?

'No,' he said. 'Horace is in the markets now. That Mr Summerbee retired through ill health and he's moving to someplace down south – Bournemouth, I think.'

But all in all, the job was OK. See, I really quite like having something interesting to do – just so long as it doesn't involve too much hard work, as such. Or as long as I can keep a good distance between me and thugs like Pudding.

I had to admit, it was a nice change not having to worry about which tourist my next wallet was coming from.

Kenny Madigan the fool in paradise.

6

All the stuff I've told you about explains how I came to be standing in Tesco's car-park looking down the barrel of a gun. Something told me that my comfortable life was about to be shattered.

A sodding gun, for Christ's sake. I hate guns in general. But to have one pointed at me – I'll never know how I managed to avoid pissing myself.

The black shape spoke. It was a sneering kind of voice, high but male.

'Tough shit, mate! You've been set up. Take two steps backward – carefully – and don't try anything stupid.'

We agreed about one thing at least: that it would be stupid of me to try anything. I backed off and he climbed out of the boot, without letting the dangerous end of his weapon wander off its target. When he stood in front of me I could tell that he was a short figure – well, shorter than me – in a dark-coloured bomber jacket, but his face was just a lighter patch of darkness.

'You better do exactly what I tell you – no heroics,' he said. There and then I made a decision – secret, like – inside my head. I would do exactly what he told me. It seemed we were about to change places, Bomber Jacket and me. So, following instructions, I started to clamber into the boot of the car. And I don't know if I finished doing that because everything went black about then.

Dim light from someplace high up. Throbbing head. Mouth like a Sumo wrestler's armpit. Bursting bladder. Must be Sunday morning . . . no, it can't be. Look around. I'm lying on a pile of dirty sacks. Looks like an unused storeroom. I totter to my feet and learn to walk. Bare plasterboard walls. Glass panels on two sides, high, out of reach, letting in second-hand daylight. And a solid-looking door that doesn't open when I turn the handle. The empty keyhole shows me another blank wall about six feet away. Nothing encouraging.

Check myself. OK except for the sore head with its new lump at the back. All the usual cargo seems to be still in my pockets. Even my wallet, where I carefully carry no identification when working . . . even that still has the two twenties I got out of the ATM yesterday. I suppose it was yesterday.

I heard myself groaning with the effort of trying to get my brain working. Who was my new acquaintance of last night, and what did he want with me? He was certainly no great conversationalist. But then I've got this theory that anybody who points a gun at somebody else immediately starts talking like Dirty Harry – they can't help it.

There was definitely something very strange going on. Even in my fuddled state, I could see that nobody hides in the boot of a car on the off-chance that it will get nicked. So I must have been expected. But how did he know . . . and why would anybody . . . Ooh, just trying to think about it made my brain hurt even more until it seized up like a gearbox with an oil leak. It was like the time my mate Steve – did I mention he worked for a bookie when he first left school? – the time he tried to tell me how to

50

calculate the odds on a triple roll-up, or something. The kind of mind I've got, you see, is suited to more sort of creative stuff and suchlike.

Suddenly I thought about Aileen. Christ, she must be worried sick. And Quinn. It looked like he had lost a motor. Maybe somebody was trying to ruin his operation. I decided right there that I was going to have nothing more to do with it. It's one thing to get a bit of a thrill outwitting the police; but when I find myself facing the wrong end of a gun I'd rather stay on the cowardly side of the street. I don't want unnecessary holes in my skin; no amount of money could be enough for that. I decided my first priority was to get out of there and start seeking unemployment.

My creative thinking was interrupted by the sound of a door opening some distance away. Then there were heavy footsteps getting nearer. Sounded like more than one set. By the time I heard a key turning in the door of my cell, I was pretending to be still out cold on the pile of sacks. Back where I had spent the night. The feet noises came up close, and a voice said, 'Stir him up, Lionel.'

The shoe that poked me none too gently in the stomach must have been about a size fifteen. I groaned and 'woke up', trying to look even more groggy than I felt. When I sat up, I could see three sets of trouser legs. The vermin were out in force. The nearest legs belonged to my prodder, and they went up a long way. This must be Lionel. His height and bulk didn't leave much room for background, but when he stepped aside I got a look at a well-dressed gent with greying hair and a natty line in bespoke tailoring. The Boss, I guessed. The third member of the committee, hanging back by the door with a twisted grin, was Bomber Jacket, my little gun-toting friend from last night.

'Take this unprepossessing specimen out and get the cobwebs off him.'

That was the Boss talking to Lionel, who grabbed my arm and yanked me to my feet. He propelled me out of the door and down a cluttered corridor to a washroom that could have supplied cobwebs wholesale. Lionel guarded the door while I used the facilities and splashed cold water over my face. Then it was back to the boudoir, where Lionel encouraged me to sit down on the pile of sacks while they lined up facing me. The Boss gave me a look that reminded me of Aileen when she's about to ask some awkward questions.

'You've caused us more trouble than you're worth, Mr Madigan,' he said, nodding slightly. There was no answer to that, so I kept quiet. He went on:

'Your assigned task was to take that car straight to Mr Quinn's premises. But, oh no, you have to be greedy and do your own private search for booty before delivering it to your employer.'

Here was something I could answer.

'I don't work for Quinn any more. I've just resigned.'

It didn't help. He grinned an evil grin at me and said, dead sarcastic like:

'I admire your loyalty. However, you misled poor Mozzer here.' He nodded towards the little bloke I thought of as Bomber Jacket. Mozzer seemed to be very interested in the proceedings. Lionel, on the other hand, just stood there trying to prevent his eyes merging together. The Boss was still talking.

'My strategy called for Mozzer to be inside Mr Quinn's security arrangements when the car stopped. You nobbled my Trojan Horse, Mr Madigan.'

'What?' I asked. He lost me there for a minute.

'Never mind. Here's what you're going to do for me. Tonight we'll all go to Lone Harp Auto, and you'll take us in that back door using your key and that security code that you have. Until then, you stay here, where I know you're secure. All right?'

'No!' I protested. 'You don't have to do that. I'll tell you the code, and you can let me go.'

He just laughed at that.

'Not a very clever try, Mr Madigan. We shall require your presence in order to ensure you're telling the truth. You'll come to no harm. Lionel here will look in a couple of times in the course of the day to bring you some food and let you go to the lavatory.'

'What happens to me afterwards?' I asked.

He used the evil grin again.

'So long as you behave yourself, you won't get hurt. It's the organ-grinder I'm interested in – not the monkey. Of course, if you make any more trouble for me, I might just let Lionel work you over. He's very competent with a tyre lever – and he enjoys exercising his skills.'

Bloody hell, my prospects were getting worse all the time. As you know, I'm a very even-tempered person, normally, but at that moment I felt I'd taken as much as I could stand. Something snapped. I jumped to my feet and yelled:

'You lousy bastard. What have I ever done to you? Some day I'll get you for this.'

I just stood there quivering with anger. The Boss didn't answer me. His voice was quiet and calm when he said:

'Let him have it, Mozzer.'

I sat down quickly, as Mozzer with a vicious smirk reached inside his bomber jacket. Oh Christ, this is it, I thought; I never did get round to fixing that bookshelf for Aileen. My brain cells were holding a strike meeting; this kind of stuff wasn't in their job description.

Mozzer's hand appeared holding something triangular, which he tossed down beside me. My brain cells still hadn't agreed to go back to work, so it was a few moments before I recognised this object as a shrink-wrapped sandwich; the kind you get in convenience stores at petrol stations. The sandwich was followed by a plastic carton of orange juice.

The Boss was laughing at me, but I didn't really care. I was thinking that I would have disgraced myself then, if I hadn't just been to the loo. But it wasn't over yet. The Boss was talking again.

'While we're here, Mr Madigan, you might as well tell us everything you know about Quinn's nefarious activities.'

I shrugged.

'Well, he gives me the gen on the cars he wants nicked, and I – '

'Not that, you fool. We know all about the car-stealing scam – and that Mickey Mouse antiques hobby of his. But what I'm interested in is the important stuff. Tell me how he does it.'

Why do I never seem to know what's going on? I just shook my head, lost for words.

'Come on,' he said. 'I'll give you a start. It's a very smart operation. The straight car business pays for the car theft set-up, which in turn provides working capital for the jewel in his crown. All I need now is to get the lowdown on his markets so I can shut him down for good.'

'I only know about nicking cars,' I said, hoping I sounded as sincere as I really was.

The Boss gave me a disgusted look.

'I haven't got time right now to wring it out of you. But we'll get the whole story tonight when we get at his records.

'Let's go.' This to his team with a jerk of his head, and they filed out of the door. As the key turned in the lock, the Boss called out to me:

'Have a nice day, Mr Madigan.'

And the footsteps clumped away down the corridor.

I peeled the sandwich open. Cheese and chutney. I hate cheese and chutney. I decided it just wasn't my day.

7

I sighed and stood up. They thought they were incredibly smart, the Boss gang. But if they had really been on the ball they would have taken the precaution of emptying my pockets. I got out my little pouch of car-nicking tools. They weren't really designed for picking this kind of lock – but they would do the job well enough.

In the corridor I turned left following the direction the foot-steps took when they went. There was another door to deal with before I reached the open air, and that took me a while, but I made it in spite of the drum that was still banging away inside my head.

After a few deep breaths of fresh air and a walk along the street to look at the nearest road signs, I worked out that I was in an industrial estate in Alcester. Eventually I managed to scrounge a lift in a builder's lorry heading towards Stratford. My first port of call was at Tesco's car-park, where I found my own car just as I had left it. After that my number one task – the thing that had to be done before I'd ever be able to sleep again – was to peel myself loose from Quinn's set-up.

Quinn was stomping around the workshop, giving everybody a hard time, when I finally got there about ten thirty.

Before I could say a word, he turned on me.

'At last. Madigan, what the fuck time do you call this? Do you think I'm paying you to lie rotting in your bed half the day?'

He wouldn't have said that if I had brought last night's car in. I ignored him, and made for the office. It made a nice change, knowing that he would have to follow me. I sat down and waited for Quinn to shut the door and get behind his desk – then I told him firmly:

'I've had enough. You can stuff your bloody job ... both of them in fact.'

His chubby face froze; the moustache twitched once and then seemed to be crouching, ready to pounce.

As usual, he ignored what I said. He came out with:

'I'm getting the feeling that something's happened ... am I right?'

I thought, Very clever, it must have taken all your brain power to work that out.

But I didn't say it; sarcasm never seems to work for me. Instead, I sighed and gave him the whole story. Well, except the bit about making an unofficial stop at my car. I said I'd heard a noise from the direction of the boot, and stopped at Tesco's car-park to investigate. When I got to telling about my discussion with Lionel, Mozzer and the Boss, Quinn's moustache came back to life. For a minute I thought it was trying to escape from his face ... I wouldn't blame it.

He wanted to know where I had been imprisoned – the exact location and how to get to it. He was also dead interested in everything about the Boss gang. Names, descriptions, what did their voices sound like, how long since their last haircuts – everything. And I found I was coming up with things I didn't know I'd noticed. You know, the Boss's suit was blue pinstripe, and single-breasted; Lionel's shoes were black lace-ups; Mozzer's bad breath – that kind of stuff.

After that, I wanted to steer the conversation back to the subject of my resignation. I took a deep breath, and Quinn's hand came up in front of my face, palm towards me.

'Hang on just one more minute, Kenny-me-boy.'

He jumped up and opened the door, yelling for Peasel. When the lad appeared, Quinn flipped a ten-pound note at him, saying:

'Wash your hands and get yourself down to Marks and Spencer's. Bring a bundle of sandwiches for Kenny, here. Sure he's had nothing to eat for a month.'

As Peasel turned to go, I remembered the sandwich Mozzer brought me. I shouted:

'Don't get any cheese and chutney.'

Quinn shut the door and came back. 'Right!' he said, sitting down. 'Now, Kenny, I can't let you run out on me, just when things are going so well.'

I couldn't believe it.

'Going well! Weren't you listening? I was kidnapped at gunpoint by a gang of nutters. Our BMW got nicked. And you think that's good? I suppose it would have been even better if I'd got shot!'

'Nothing but a hiccup,' he said. 'You just leave it to me. I know how to sort out evil bastards like them. Have I ever let you down? By the way, you still get your money for the BMW job . . . pick it up at the usual place.'

'No,' I said, all determined, 'I'm finished. I don't need your kind of trouble. You better find somebody else to nick cars.'

Quinn showed me his teeth. The moustache was purring now. All the outward signs belonged to the pleasant, charming side of my boss; but for some reason I felt a wave of apprehension washing over me. I shivered, probably because of my recent ordeal. Quinn leaned forward and spoke softly:

'You don't seem to understand me, Kenny-me-lad. You haven't got any choice on account of you're in this business up to your balls. As you know, I'm kindness itself to the guys on my side, but I can turn very nasty indeed when somebody on my own team crosses me up. I would really hate it if you were to be seriously maimed, and have to spend months in plaster, just when I need you the most.'

There it was – a definite threat. It hung there between us like a small cloud above the desk. Angus's warning came into my mind. What was it he said? – 'Yon Quinn is a fucking dangerous man . . .'

All at once I recognised my shiver for what it was. I was more scared than when Mozzer pointed his gun at me. At least you know where you are with the enemy; but this was a stab in the back out of the blue. I nibbled on my left thumbnail where I'd split it working on the lock; it seemed the most important thing for me to be doing just then.

Quinn was having one of his silences – just sitting there looking at me. Oh, well . . . maybe something would come up. I didn't want to hear any more about maiming, so I changed the subject.

'What was all that stuff about the antiques they were asking me?'

I didn't feel up to telling Quinn that the Boss thought he was up to something stronger than nicking cars – it sounded as if it might be too, you know, private.

Quinn's eyebrows joined his moustache in a little dance, and the tension drained away.

'Well, sure. Antiques is my other business right enough. Before you ask, it's legal. What the hell did you think I use the other section of this building for?'

I played dumb and pretended to be puzzled. He probably didn't know that Scheri had mentioned the antique furniture to me. I said:

'Do you mean you keep antiques in there? Your shop must be somewhere else then.'

His eyes joined in the grin that was left over from his threatening expression.

'All right,' he said, 'I suppose you've earned the right to know a bit about it. I like to keep things in their own airtight boxes. So none of the fellas in the car business know about the antiques – remember that. I take myself around the country picking up English antiques in auctions and house clearances. Mostly furniture and sometimes the odd bit of porcelain, that kind of stuff.'

Quinn was back on his friendly track again, explaining how busy he kept himself.

'That's the reason why I'm away so much of the time. The furniture I buy gets hauled into the warehouse here; and when there's enough to fill a forty-foot container, I ship it over to Randy Haines, my buddy in Dallas. There's antique malls an' stores all over the Metroplex. The dealers over there can't get enough of that crap.'

I nodded, thinking it sounded like a good business idea . . . but there must be more to it than that. I frowned.

'But I never see any signs of life in the warehouse; and it's right here in this building, so you'd think we would hear the sounds of furniture arriving and leaving, even though the entrance is round the back.'

'That's easy. The guy who drives my truck works for somebody else in the daytime, so all the deliveries come in at night. OK?'

The sincerity in Quinn's eyes was being poured out so strong that I didn't believe a word of it. He went on as if an idea had just struck him:

'Now that you know about it, maybe you can help me out in the antiques side of the outfit. Sure I'll give that serious consider- ation, Kenny. I just bet you and that lovely lady of yours could find a use for some extra money.'

That was a mistake, that last bit. I suddenly got a different view of Quinn. Now he was sounding just like every manage- ment I ever worked for. Trying to butter me up and getting it wrong. They always think that vague promises of money are the right carrot to keep me eating out of their hands.

Bastards! I said nothing.

'Right!' he grinned. 'Now we understand each other. You take the rest of the day off. Leave these scumbags to me. I know how to deal with arseholes who try to muscle in on my operation. There won't be any more trouble from that neck of the woods.'

I wasn't going to commit to anything. I needed to think. So I just left without another word. On my way out I got my bundle of sandwiches from Peasel, back from his mission to Marks and Spencer's. As I got into my car, I suddenly started to feel like a used tea-bag. Must have been the effects of my ordeal catching up with me. What with that and the blinding headache I had from being clubbed by Mozzer, it would be nice to get home and have a good sleep till Aileen got in from work.

I parked in the street outside the maisonette, and walked upstairs thinking about nothing else but getting my head down. Half- way up, the Neighbourhood Witch barred my way, elbows at a businesslike angle.

'Good morning, Miss Downie,' I said. It was still morning – just about.

'You've just missed your friend,' she said, loud enough to be heard in Anne Hathaway's cottage about a mile away. It wasn't just the volume that got my attention. I tried to look questioningly at her, but it wasn't necessary; she was screeching on anyway.

'I found him at your door. He said he had come to return the iron bar he was holding, that he borrowed from you. I said you would be at your work, and he could safely leave it with me, but he said no, he really needed to see you, so he would wait till he could let you have it personally – he's a big lad, isn't he, reminds me of my sister Daisy's boy. Well dressed and all. I always think a really tall man looks so much better in a proper blue suit, don't you – '

'All right, Miss Downie,' I broke in. 'Thanks for letting me know. I expect you'll be wanting to get back to your broomstick now. Have a sandwich.' I shoved a tuna mayonnaise triangle into her hand.

'What?' she bawled. I felt ashamed of myself for my insult to the dreadful old baggage. It was actually the result of my new surge of fear, but it had the right effect. She was puzzled for long enough to let me slip past and get to my own door.

As I was putting my key into the lock, I got the blast of Miss Downie's parting shot.

'Anyways, he said to tell you that Lionel was here, and he'll be getting in touch soon. Thanks for the sarnie.'

Knackered as I was, I couldn't sleep. There was just too much going on in my life and in my head – none of it helpful, as such. So I just lay there reviewing my options – not that I seemed to have any.

Would Quinn really have me beaten up if I stopped working for him? I remembered Pudding and what happened to Mr Summerbee; and I shuddered a bit under the duvet. No – Quinn wouldn't let me off the hook, especially now that I was getting to know more about his various businesses.

And then there was the Boss and Lionel and Mozzer. These

nutters were not really interested in me. They only wanted to use me as a way of getting at Quinn.

But wait a minute; they would be after me anyway. They would never believe I knew nothing, even if I got out of the Quinn thing. So maybe I should stick with the devil I knew. Quinn, that is. Who knows, maybe he wasn't kidding when he said he could protect me from the other lot.

There was so much going on that I didn't understand. I decided this was one time when my policy of ignorance had stopped being useful, and my best chance of protection might be to know as *much* as possible. I started to make a list, just in my head, like, while I was lying there not sleeping. All the questions; all the mysteries. Not many answers.

What kind of business could Quinn be in that was more dangerous than recycling cars? And why was the Boss so interested? I decided that Quinn must somehow have stepped on the Boss's toes – muscled in on his territory, or something.

How did the Boss gang know what car I was going to nick, so that Mozzer could hide in it? Inside information. OK, but where from? They could have followed me and noted what car I was interested in; then got Mozzer into position when they realised I was about to make the pick-up. Anyone at Lone Harp would know when I was doing one of my 'little jobs' for Quinn, even if they didn't know what it was.

And then there was Quinn's secret antiques business. If it was as straight as he said, there was no need to hide it. Maybe it could be a cover for some other activity, just like the garage was a cover for the car-stealing operation. The only thing I could think of was that it might have something to do with drugs. No particular reason for thinking that; it was just that drugs are big business and very profitable for the pond life who deal in them. And another thing, the drug trade causes a lot of trouble between rival gangs. On the other hand, the Boss had seemed to think the antiques business was of no importance. I put the drug idea aside for now, but filed it as a possible.

How deep was Scheri involved in it? Right up to her neck, I guessed – and that was a long way up. I already knew that she fingered the cars to be nicked.

Then I remembered the stuff I'd seen on Scheri's computer screen – you know, the Edwardian desk and all that other furniture. So Scheri was at the centre of the antiques thing as well. I came back to wondering if she was maybe the real boss of the whole Quinn empire.

Anyway, the only conclusion I could come to was that I should find out as much as I could about what was going on. It was the only way I could think of to protect my skin. I believe I've already mentioned how important it is for me to keep myself unhurt.

There seemed to be two ways to go from here; and I decided to do both of them. One was to find out more about the Quinn set-up – the organisation I would have to go on working for till there was a safe exit. No more of the Angus-style attitude that says, 'I do my tiny bit and don't want to know anything else.'

The other avenue I might explore was more dangerous on the face of it – the Boss and his two little helpers. I didn't know a thing about them, except that they were definitely not local. My guess was London, based on the kind of accent sported by both Lionel and Mozzer. Not to mention the dead polite voice of the Boss himself. It should be possible to find out something about them. Maybe I could watch outside the warehouse in Alcester and follow them when they left – or at least follow the Boss.

I must have drifted off to sleep about then, because the next thing I knew was Aileen's voice raised in a very annoyed way. Much as I love Aileen, I've got to admit that when she gets agitated she can sound like chalk on a squeaky blackboard.

Anyway, I made up some story about having got stuck out in the wilds, and not being able to find a phone that hadn't been vandalised. I decided that she didn't need to know all about my latest batch of problems. For her own safety – or at least that was what I told myself. But I was so doom-laden that I couldn't bring myself to smile for her.

I wouldn't say that Aileen didn't believe my story; I can never tell whether she believes me or not. See, if she disapproves of whatever I've done, she still goes on at me even though she knows I'm telling the truth. So what I did was, I tried to pull her into bed. Sex is sometimes the only treatment that will shut her up – and I was feeling a lot more healthy after my sleep. It would have taken my mind off my troubles for a short time at least.

It didn't work this time though; she avoided my advances and still ranted on and forced me to eat some vile health food tablets

– porcupine quill essence or something. So I just switched off, and all I can remember is the last sentence before she actually shut up, as such.

'... and if you ever do anything like that again, Kendall Madigan, you'll find yourself bonking your fist for the next month at least.'

She must have been really upset. Aileen's usually careful not to be coarse. Still, what about me; my whole world falling apart, and I couldn't even get a bit of nookie to forget my problems.

Kenny Madigan the celibated Stratford monk.

8

Aileen microwaved some spaghetti bolognaise out of the freezer for dinner, but I couldn't eat very much on account of my brain cells were concentrating on the planning of my next move. I was going to wait till late, and then go out on what I was beginning to think of as my first investigation. Aileen wasn't too curious, because by this time she was used to my erratic working hours, and had a policy of not knowing too much about what I was doing. She was pretty damn keen on spending the extra money, though.

I forced myself to sit beside Aileen on the sofa watching television, in spite of being all revved up, ready to go, like. The noise from the programmes didn't help, either. See, Aileen's got this impatient attitude to television; if nobody on the screen says anything for about five seconds, she uses the remote control to turn up the volume – as if that could make them talk. And she insists on being in control of the remote. The last thing I needed just then was to be deafened by the police sirens in *The Bill*.

Aileen went off to bed about eleven, and I thought I would wait another hour before slipping out. I was intending to go through with my half-baked idea of trailing one or more members of the Boss gang. However, as it happened, I was saved from that piece of stupidity by the phone ringing. Though what I got into instead was probably a lot worse.

It was Quinn on the phone, sounding very souped up.

'Come on, Kenny, you and me are going out to that warehouse where they took you last night. I'll be round to pick you up in ten minutes. Be ready – and bring a flashlight . . . oh, and them lock-picking tools of yours.'

'You don't need me,' I said. 'I've told you exactly how to get there. It's no problem.'

But it was no use protesting. He was in a mood to roll right over any objections.

'Look,' he said, 'there isn't time to argue with you. I hate women having to get hurt, but if you care about that Aileen of yours, you'll shut your mouth and do as I say.'

I decided to shut my mouth, but I wasn't able to shut down the scary feeling I had about going back to that place. What if Mozzer and the rest of the Boss gang were in residence? Anyway, five minutes later I was out in the street waiting for Quinn's Vauxhall Calibra. On the ten-mile journey to Alcester he drove as if he could hardly keep the wheels on the ground. Luckily the roads were quiet at that time of night. Quinn obviously didn't need directions to the warehouse that had been my prison. It was in a little industrial estate spread out on both sides of a road that was put there just to give access to the workshops and warehouses.

Quinn parked some distance down the road from the warehouse where there were some other cars. Again, he didn't seem to need directions from me. That was when I formed a distinct impression that this was not the first time he had been here.

The warehouse was in darkness, as I had been hoping. Whatever was kept here couldn't be important enough to need a night-watchman. The door in the side of the building where I had made my escape was shut, of course. My little tool kit in its leather pouch should handle that without too much trouble.

Quinn had his own flashlight. He held its beam on the lock while I chose the right combination of tools. But we didn't need them. As soon as I touched the door, it swung open with a loud creak. My first thought was that maybe somebody was already inside; why else would the door be open? But there was no glimmer of light, so I decided that it must have been left open by the last person to leave. Quinn led the way in and I pushed the door shut behind us; another loud creak struck me as less of a problem than the risk of somebody reporting an open door.

The wide corridor inside looked dead sinister by the light of our two torches; what with the weird shadows cast by the lumps of wood and empty crates that lined one wall. I followed a cautious three paces behind Quinn.

The first door, about six yards down on the right, was standing open. It belonged to a room I knew only too bloody well. This was where I spent an unpleasant night through no fault of my own. I had no intention of going back in there if I could help it, but Quinn stopped beside it and whispered:

'It looks empty from here ... but go in and check it out anyway. I'll go on down this corridor.'

Not being into perverted nostalgia, I was pretty reluctant but came up with what I thought of as a compromise:

'No, you stay there and cover me with that torch.'

I took one step in and gave the room a quick sweep with my light, intending to get out within about three seconds. I held the beam for a moment on the famous pile of sacks. Then I wished I hadn't bothered. There was a hand – yes, *again* – poking out from under the sacks.

I had a sudden vision of the hand that had spooked me in the boot – and for some reason it made me furious. Did they think they could catch me out the same way twice? They must have been expecting us, I thought, without much logic. Whatever the reason, I wasn't going to be taken in by it this time. I tiptoed back to where Quinn was waiting and lit up my face to let him see my finger on my lips. He stood silent while I went a few steps down the corridor, and picked up a piece of two-by-two about three feet long. Gripping the wood in both hands, I let Quinn light my way as I went back into the storeroom and brought my club down as hard as I could, on the shape beneath the sacks. Just about where the head should be.

That did it for me. My anger drained away, and I remembered how much I hate violence. Though in a way I was excited by having struck a blow for the good guys at last.

I drop the piece of wood, and pull the sacks aside. Quinn is beside me now. No surprise. It's Mozzer, lying face up on the bare concrete floor. And he isn't moving. In fact, he seems unnaturally still. Surely I didn't hit him hard enough to ...? It's quite chilly in that room, all of a sudden.

He can't be dead. But I feel alone in spite of the quiet man beside me. My heart is hammering. My legs have gone a bit rubbery. That makes it easy for me to kneel down. I force myself to feel for a pulse. Nothing! And Mozzer feels colder than he should. Not icy cold, exactly. But colder than you expect a living human being to be. I hold down the panic ... point my light at his head. My wooden club struck just about there. I don't find a bruise. But a small black hole in the middle of Mozzer's forehead is expanding to fill my whole universe. No blood can be seen.

So I hadn't killed Mozzer with my piece of wood. That was a kind of relief. I would hate to be a murderer, no matter how nasty the murderee might be. But he was dead, all the same. For a while I was paralysed with the horror of finding a body – one who had been shot by somebody else. Inside my head, a suspicion was rising through all the horror to sit right on the surface.

'Pull yourself together, Kenny.' Quinn spoke at last. 'Is this one of the guys who held you here?'

The spell was broken and I managed a nod, forgetting that it couldn't be seen.

After a moment's silence Quinn said, 'Sure and he's dead all right. It looks like we're not the only ones he's offended. It's lucky I'm with you, or you might be a suspect. Don't touch a thing. You stay here while I check the rest of the place.'

I waited – but outside in the corridor, as Quinn went off to do a check through the rest of the building. There was a chill feeling in my bones, though my brain cells were getting back to work. Don't touch a thing, he said, but I must have already left fingerprints in various parts of this building. The police had no record of me; I knew that. Still, who knows whether they might somehow connect me with Mozzer – and then it wouldn't take them long to get my dabs and compare them with any they could find in the warehouse. My heart jumped as I remembered something I had seen without quite registering it – Quinn was wearing gloves.

Well, there was something I could do to safeguard myself. When Quinn got back having found nothing, there I was, busy using an old bucket from the dirty washroom, and a wet sack, wiping the walls and door of the storeroom by the fading light of my torch. I made sure to wipe every place I might have touched in that storeroom. Then he waited while I wiped the washroom taps, the cistern handle and the piece of wood I'd hit Mozzer with.

'Well done,' Quinn said. 'Now let's get out of here and keep our mouths shut.'

We got out.

Mozzer was an ugly vicious criminal, but he didn't deserve to die like that. I never even knew his real name – well, not till later. The thought of him still lying in that manky warehouse kept nagging at me like a sore tooth. So the next morning, I made a call to the police from a phone box. With my handkerchief stuffed into my mouth, I told them where to find the body. 'Who's calling?' the police operator kept asking – as if there was some chance of an answer.

Funny thing though, I never heard any report of Mozzer's murder on the radio, or in any of the local or national newspapers, though I kept on the look-out for a good week. One local paper printed a short article about hoax calls wasting police time. It mentioned there had even been a recent anonymous call reporting a non-existent dead body.

Thinking about it, I came to the conclusion that Mozzer's mates must have come back to the warehouse, discovered him deceased, and removed the corpse. I supposed they would have dumped it where it wouldn't be found. Or at least where it wouldn't draw attention to a place they were using.

As for who killed him, I could think of three possibilities. It could have been one of his own gang, if they'd had a fall-out. Or it might have been someone else that I didn't know; people like Mozzer must have a lot of enemies. But I was really kidding myself. I knew in my heart that Quinn had been there earlier that night – and that I had been taken there to find the body and give him an alibi if he ever needed one. I heard his voice again in my mind:

'Leave these scumbags to me. I know how to deal with arseholes who try to muscle in on my operation.'

I suppose in a way he did it for me. No, that wasn't right; he was only interested in protecting his own twisted interests. I was just an innocent prawn in his game – well, fairly innocent – who had got swept into something nasty through no fault of my own, and couldn't think of a way to sweep myself out of it. Still, Quinn was right when he said I was in it right up to my balls. I could go to the police and tell them everything I knew, but that would mean putting myself in the frame for all these car thefts. I filed that possibility away for now. I might be driven to it if things kept on getting worse.

There was one thing that my watching of the papers turned up – you know, when I was looking for news of Mozzer. Something that chilled me to the bladder. It was a report of the unidentified dead body of a man that was found in bushes at the side of a road in Redditch. He had died of knife wounds and was apparently dumped from a car during the night. It said the corpse was that of a white male about thirty-five years old with an army-style haircut. He was wearing a grey T-shirt and one ear-ring. So that definitely wasn't Mozzer. The police expected to make an early arrest – but they always say that.

I never saw Pudding after that. Nobody I knew ever mentioned him. That corpse could have been me if I hadn't been smart enough – or lucky enough – to escape from the Boss's clutches.

There was no doubt in my mind that I had been close to a pair of tit-for-tat murders.

My Auntie Ursula used to have a saying: 'Where the river bends, the blind man falls in.'

Right now, I felt like that blind man – and Quinn was certainly as bent as any river; he could hide behind a spiral staircase.

In the end, I decided to keep to my policy of finding out as much as possible about the whole set-up. Not that I had actually got round to doing anything about it yet. There was still that threat of Quinn's hanging over me and Aileen – and I had no reason to believe that it would go away all by itself.

So I was still stuck in a hell of a diabolical situation. My Auntie Ursula would have sniffed and told me:

'You've made your bed, and you can lie in it.'

But that would be saying it was my fault.

You and I know that none of it was my fault.

9

Meanwhile, I went on working at Lone Harp Auto. There didn't seem to be anything else I could do. Quinn never said another word about my abduction or that horrible night when we went back to the place in Alcester. But he seemed to have changed – or maybe it was my view of him that had changed. Often he would stand at his office door watching the workshop at work, and to the blokes working there he was just a reasonably decent boss who might lose his rag with them occasionally, but OK, that's his privilege. But for me it was different. I could feel the malice radiating from him. And I got a lump of dread deep inside.

Two weeks went by without any activity on the car-stealing front. I also got the impression that there were not as many faceless visitors as before. In line with my policy of finding out as much as I could, I took up Scheri's long-standing invitation. I sometimes went in the back office for coffee with her at times when things were slack in the workshop, but only on days when Quinn was not around.

I was only concerned with getting information. Honest. Though I have to admit that I enjoyed Scheri's company. She was different from any other woman I knew – more . . . frank, I suppose – not the least embarrassed about being sexy, and always ready to flaunt it a bit. I think she enjoyed making me feel uncomfortable. Like when she leaned over to pour coffee into my mug she would keep that blouseful of breasts hovering in my face longer than necessary. Not that I'm complaining, you understand.

As for the idea of getting information, these sessions were about as useful as tits on a nun. I got plenty of useless information from Scheri; mostly about the differences between living in England and America, with special reference to Texas, which seemed to be superior to all the other forty-nine states. Still, I kept my eyes open, and watched what was going on with the computers – not that it meant much to me.

Once while I was there, though, the computer seemed to be working away, with lots of flickering on the screen. Every now and again the flickering would stop and the machine would bleep, with a message on the screen that said, 'Insert diskette 4,' and next time diskette 5, and so on. Each time it did that Scheri would turn round to change the little square diskette doodah that fits in the slot at the front of the computer. I asked her:

'What's going on here? Why do you need to keep changing over?'

'Just doing a backup run,' she replied. 'You never can tell when your hard disk might go belly-up. So I make a copy of all the vital data every week. That way, I could never lose more than a week's work.'

'I see,' I lied. 'That gives you an extra copy of all the programs.'

'No, honey, just the data. Programs I can reinstall from the original diskettes or CD Roms – right?'

I nodded wisely and gave up trying to understand. My mate Steve would have known what was going on. But I watched carefully, and noted where she kept the backup diskettes. They went into a little plastic box with a see-through lid. Maybe I could ask Steve to explain.

In the meantime, I tried another subject:

'I suppose you and Quinn must have met up when he was in America?'

'We sure did,' she said.

'Was that when he was working in the car factory?'

'The Buick plant ... yeah, he worked there for a few years when he first came over. He had an older brother who had emigrated to the USA some years earlier, so when Quinn got fed up with the dead-end hick town where he was raised, he just naturally went to join his brother.'

'So there's two of them.' I was surprised.

'No, they had a falling out a few years back. Quinn walked out on his brother and his job at Buick. That was when he discovered the advantages of working against the system.'

'Even so,' I said, 'why would he want to come here to open up shop? I mean, if he was doing OK in Texas or wherever?'

Scheri seemed to be embarrassed, kind of.

'Mmm ... well ...' she said slowly, 'he has his reasons. Let's just say it seemed like a good idea for him to be someplace else for a while.'

I nodded. 'OK, I suppose that explains why Quinn's here. But what about you? What made you come with him?'

Scheri surprised me by looking a bit . . . well, sad.

'Yeah, for a while I thought I was going to be free . . . that is, I thought I was getting rid of him for a while at least. But nobody gets rid of Quinn that easy once he's got his claws . . . Look, I've said too much. Just forget we had this conversation, OK?'

She forced a smile back on to her face and looked straight at me without blinking. I don't think I've ever seen anybody look so dead vulnerable, as such.

'What conversation?' I said.

Trouble kept its head down, as I said, for two weeks. Then in the third week, I got another car-nicking job. Quinn and Scheri handed it out, as usual, seated behind the big desk. Scheri was always strictly businesslike at these times. In fact, she was never the least bit familiar when Quinn was around. These little sessions when they fingered a car for me to nick, they were always dead formal. I always felt they should come out with some corny line like:

'Here, should you decide to accept it, is your next assignment.'

Only I didn't get the choice of accepting or rejecting it, of course.

This one was a white Mercedes – one of the big ones. It was located in Sambourne, out towards Redditch.

Well, I did my usual professional job, and the whole thing went pretty smoothly – until the journey home in the Merc. I'd come round the Alcester bypass, taking it smooth and easy, and quite enjoying the luxurious feel of the big silent motor. It was about 2 a.m. on a fine clear night, so there was very little traffic – just a pair of headlights a long way behind. Ahead, I watched a car come out of a side road and turn towards Stratford. It didn't accelerate very much, and, as I caught up, the whole back of that car lit up like a sodding Christmas tree.

POLICE, it said. Below that it said STOP, and the STOP was flashing on and off. Bloody traffic police. Why weren't they in Stratford putting tickets on all the cars parked on double yel-

70

lows? The police car went into a lay-by, obviously intending me to follow. I had a wild thought of doing a runner. The Mercedes could certainly outrun a police Vauxhall Omega. I gave up the idea. Communications are so good these days that they would have had a road block ahead of me in minutes; and if I took to the twisty country lanes, I wouldn't be able to go fast enough to get away from the Omega.

I drove meekly into the lay-by and stopped a few yards behind the coppers. The Christmas tree was switched off, and a dark-suited figure with a cap on got out of the police car's passenger side. As he walked towards me, I was wondering what the hell I would say. If we were in a TV police series, it would be something like:

'You got me bang to rights, guv. It's a fair cop. I'll come quietly.'

On the whole, not a good idea. The flock of bats swooping about in my intestines would very likely make a shaky job of *anything* I might say. When the copper was close, I pressed the button that lowers the window. I sat there looking up at him as if I was a solid citizen, puzzled about being stopped by the police. Luckily, the intestinal bats prevented me saying:

'Lovely night, officer. How can I help you?'

That's the kind of line the real owner of my Mercedes would get in that TV show.

The policeman leaned forward and stuck his head through the window (they do that to see if they can catch a whiff of alcohol on your breath). I swear you could have knocked me over with a parrot when he said:

'Good evening, sir. Sorry to trouble you, but there's somebody who would like to have a quiet word. If you'll just remain here for a moment, please.'

He said *please*! A copper said *please* to me! Thank Christ he didn't salute – that would have been really nasty.

What with all this police stuff taking place, I hadn't noticed what else was happening. Now I caught a flash of light in my rear-view mirror, and realised that a new punter had come into the game. Another car was now stopped ten yards behind the Mercedes. I remembered the headlights which were following me earlier. Whatever was going on, I was willing to bet that it was definitely not ·intended for my comfort and convenience. I watched the uniform go back to his car, which moved off and faded down the road towards Stratford. The bats were still with me, though.

Next thing I knew, the front passenger door of the Mercedes was yanked open, and there was a black shape filling its gap. A voice said:

'Nice car, Kenny. Mind if I join you?'

I knew that voice. It was Neil, the plain-clothes copper who was Sally's boyfriend. And there was I thinking her choice of men had improved. How wrong can you be? I decided I had jumped out of the fire, straight into the soup without a paddle.

Neil didn't wait for an invitation. He got into the car and shut the door.

'It's time you and I had a serious talk,' he said.

I opened my mouth to brazen it out, but I could only stammer, 'The car . . . about the car. I . . . I . . .'

I actually felt he was showing me a bit of mercy when he interrupted.

'It's OK, Kenny. There's no point in trying to spin me some wild story. I might have to pretend to believe it.'

Pretend to believe it! What did he mean? He went on:

'Relax. I know all about the cars. This must be . . . what? . . . getting on for about the twentieth, right?'

I was feeling really miserable now.

'So why haven't . . . why didn't . . .'

Neil finished the question for me.

'Why weren't you picked up long ago? Well, you certainly deserved to be, but you're just small fry; the people I'm after are much more important than you, people like your boss for instance . . . and some of the things they are doing are a lot worse than stealing cars, believe me. So if we pull you in, they'll know that we're on to them, and we'll lose the chance of breaking up one of the biggest organised crime rackets we've ever had in this country. Now, I don't think you're implicated in the serious stuff – you're just a pawn. But you could be useful to us.'

That was a lot for me to digest. My dearest wish was to be even smaller fry. I didn't really pay much attention to most of what he had said. I was kind of hypnotised by the spark of hope that was lurking in the middle of it.

'Do you mean you're not arresting me?'

72

I couldn't make out his face in the dark. But I heard the grin in his voice when he answered.

'You're catching on fast, Kenny. Yes, you're off the hook – for the moment anyway.'

'So why are you telling me this? Is it to stop the cars being . . . er . . . abducted?'

I could just about see Neil's head shaking from side to side.

'No, not at all. In fact I want you to carry on doing it – business as usual.'

I had to protest at this. 'No chance, mate. You wouldn't believe how seriously I want to get myself out of this game. You've just delivered the decider.'

'Sorry, Kenny, it's not as easy as that. If you stopped nicking cars now, I'm afraid I would have to think about putting you away for a while. You wouldn't enjoy wearing prison clothes. But I would rather have your whole-hearted co-operation.'

My heart sank. So did my stomach, lungs, liver and, for all I know, my spleen as well. This guy was just as unscrupulous as Quinn and the Boss gang. I was getting a glimmer of what he was after.

'So I suppose you want me to spy on Quinn and tell you everything I can find out?'

'That's the idea. I hope you haven't got any of those silly notions that a lot of criminals have. You know, like refusing to grass on your mates.'

I was indignant.

'Definitely not. I'm not really a criminal, as such. All the same, I don't know that much about Quinn and what he gets up to.'

I was quiet for a minute, wishing for some distraction that would give me time to think and work out exactly what to tell Neil.

No UFOs landed beside the car, so I ended up telling him about Quinn's antiques business. I said that it was legitimate as far as I knew. I did mention my suspicion that there was something dodgy about it – but Neil could work that out for himself from the fact that it only seemed to operate at night. He didn't sound highly impressed with my information, so I got the idea that he already knew something about the antiques. Some stuff I carefully avoided, like my kidnapping and the Boss gang and the whole Mozzer thing.

73

'All right, so you'll now be actively looking for information. I need a man on the inside, and you're all that fate has managed to come up with. Tough.'

He was quiet for a minute. Then he wheeled out another question.

'Did you ever come across a man called Percival Hopper? Posh Perce, they call him, because he's educated and well spoken. He operates out of London, though we know he has contacts everywhere. Among other things he's what we call a superfence – buys stolen valuables, sometimes even works of art, from fences all over the country, and launders them somehow.

'We know he spent some time in this area recently, along with a couple of his gorillas. We don't know why, but I don't think he was here to see *A Midsummer Night's Dream* or Anne Hathaway's cottage.'

I shook my head in the dark, thinking I had probably just put a name to the Boss. This was interesting from my point of view. I wanted to hear more.

'Never heard of him,' I said. 'Do you think he's involved with Quinn?'

'We suspect he might be. But to tell you the truth, we're just guessing. There's a rumour that your friend Quinn has done something to offend the criminal establishment; and Hopper is about as established as you can get. One of the blokes who came up here with Hopper – a vicious nutter called Mostyn – was found dead in Bognor Regis when we thought he was still in the Stratford area. His body was washed up on the beach, but he didn't drown. He died of a gunshot wound to the head. He won't be missed.'

Poor old Mozzer, I thought. I wouldn't miss him either.

Neil paused for a moment, then asked in an innocent voice, 'Is Quinn into works of art, or anything like that?'

'How would I know?' I said and hastily added, 'On the other hand, I might be able to get information about Quinn's activities. Of course, you'll have to tell me something about what's going on. Is the antiques business a cover for some kind of drugs operation?'

'Drugs?' he said. 'No, it's not drugs; it's . . . well, it's something else. You don't need to know the details. Might be dangerous for you if you did.'

74

It was hard to believe he would care about danger to me. I got the impression he didn't really know any more than I did – he was only pretending to have access to loads more information.

Neil shifted in the leather passenger seat of the Mercedes, turning sideways to face me. It was too dark to make out his expression.

'We did wonder about drugs at first, but we can't think of an angle. The USA and Britain are both at the end of the line for the drug networks – there's no percentage in transferring dope between the two markets. Then there's the antiques. There *is* a small trade in smuggling high value antiques out of the country, under false colours, so to speak – you know, the documentation describes the item as something pretty ordinary, and only an expert can tell the difference. But Quinn is shipping out large quantities of pretty cheap stuff, verging on junk. We've checked it out, and his documentation is spot-on. I'm told they can't get enough of crappy old English furniture in the States. Oh, and we got the Customs and Excise guys to search one of his containers. And they went over it with trained drug-sniffer dogs just in case. Nada. And we can't keep searching Quinn's containers unless we have good evidence. The Customs and Excise boys are well miffed at us for wasting their time.'

'So how do you know Quinn's got something dodgy going on?'

'He's a bloody villain, isn't he. Anyway, his name keeps coming up. He's caused ripples throughout criminal circles all over the country since he started up over here. So there's no doubt that he's treading on somebody's toes. Besides, he's not a man to start a business unless there's something bent about it. We know a bit about his previous form from the FBI. Apparently both he and that woman of his have been into some pretty shady stuff in the States. Also the IRS are pretty keen to get hold of him – and they strike a lot more fear into the heart of everybody in America than the FBI, the CIA and the Mafia added together.'

I wasn't surprised by anything Neil had said. He was holding something back though. Stands to reason he was only telling me what he thought I needed to know. Well, two can play at that kettle of fish. I said:

'Right, then! If I get you the goods on Quinn, you won't arrest me for nicking the cars. Have I got that straight?'

He was maybe a bit evasive, but I don't suppose I could expect anything else.

'Kenny,' he said, full of crocodile sincerity, 'if you help me nail that bastard Quinn, you'll be covered in glory – and I'll get my promotion to inspector. I was sent here to investigate the Quinn set-up, and I intend to get the evidence any way I can.'

There was no answer to that. Neil opened the car door and got out. Before shutting it, he leaned back in and said:

'I don't want to rush you, but I need results yesterday. I'll be in touch. Goodnight. Mind how you go.'

Then he was off, back to his own car. For about five minutes I sat there wondering who else could crawl out of the woodpile and apply all their efforts to turning the screw on Kenny Madigan.

Talk about a twist of fate. My life was more like a hokey-cokey of fate.

10

The only thing Neil had in common with Quinn, it seemed to me, was that they were both determined to condemn me to a permanent life of crime. My Auntie Ursula would have called it an unholy appliance. Then there's the Boss's lot – I suppose I should call him Hopper, now that I know his name. They seemed to be scared off for the moment, at least. It would be too much to expect for them to stay away, considering what Neil said about Quinn stepping on the toes of half the big-time criminals in the country. And what *about* Neil? He definitely knew a lot more than he told me. Still, even *he* was obviously not as smart as he thought he was – he didn't know that Mozzer was killed near here. And it seemed that he didn't know anything about Pudding either.

So I kept on keeping on because there wasn't anything else I could do. At least now I knew I wouldn't be nicked by the Old Bill for nicking cars. On the other hand, I was forced to get really serious in finding out more about Quinn's business activities. I decided that the antiques business would have to be my starting point. In fact, it was the only starting point I could think of. Like a great big tangled bunch of string; you have to find a loose end before you can begin to unravel it. Scheri might be as loose an end as any.

Up to then, when I was in the inner office having coffee with Scheri, I had always been careful to avoid being too friendly in case she got the idea I was interested in her – you know, sexually. For one thing, there was Quinn to consider. I hated to think what he might do to me if Scheri told him I was getting too familiar. And if Aileen ever got wind of it, my life would be even less worth living.

However, I changed my approach on our next coffee morning. There was no real plan in my head, just the idea that if I started to shake things up, something might fall out. I insisted on pouring Scheri's coffee; and put my hand on her shoulder while I did it. Then, during our conversation, which was mostly about a delivery of parts and supplies we were expecting, I didn't do my usual avoiding of eye contact. This led to us looking straight into each other's eyes quite a lot; and I don't know if this had any effect on Scheri, but it was certainly doing things to me.

Eventually, she had to make some comment. Displaying her entire collection of teeth, she said:

'It sure is nice to see you acting so friendly, Kenny. I'm starting to think that you are coming on to me.'

Angus saved me from having to think up an answer to that. He came in with a batch of workshop job sheets for costing. I made my escape with him, pretending that I had to reorganise some stock racks to make room for the new supplies.

That was a Monday. All day Tuesday and Wednesday morning, Quinn was there, making his presence felt, and sticking his oar into everything that was going on in Lone Harp Auto. He always acted as if he could do all the jobs better than the people who were getting paid to do them. Trouble is, he probably could; but it still upset the smooth running of the workshop, and made the rest of us take out our annoyance on each other.

At last, about eleven thirty on Wednesday, with everyone's nerves snapping like Yorkshire terriers, Quinn yelled to Angus:

'Right, fella, you're in charge. See you on Friday. Just keep a close eye on Jeff till he's finished that suspension job.'

Quinn didn't even wait for Angus's nodded reply. He walked

out of the workshop and drove away in his Vauxhall Calibra surrounded by a cloud of Willie Nelson. Quinn only ever drove General Motors cars – on principle, he said.

At lunch time I went into the back office. Scheri was wearing a short blue skirt instead of the usual Levis, and was showing yards of fairly spectacular leg. (I was willing to bet *she* would measure more than forty-four inches from hip to toe.) Her blonde hair was tied back, and she had on a kind of crossover blouse thing that made the foothills of her breasts look like the promised land. She stood up as I arrived and ignored my stare, which I couldn't help. With a grin she picked up the coffee jug and said:

'Hi, Kenny. Take the weight off. I'm just gonna wash this out and fill it, then I'm all yours.'

Chance would be a fine thing, I thought. Scheri left on her way to the little scullery at the back of the workshop, and I was alone for the first time in the nerve centre of Quinn's empire. I cursed myself for not knowing enough about computers. Still, there must be something to find out. There were piles of papers here and there on the tables, but they all seemed to be paperwork relating to Lone Harp Auto.

Then I caught sight of the plastic box of backup diskettes. Too late! I leapt back to my chair as I heard the door to the outer office opening. I leaned over to peer through the connecting door, which was ajar, and saw that it was only Angus, come to pick up a job sheet from the tray on Quinn's desk. He went immediately, and I was left wondering if there was still enough time for me to get to the diskettes before Scheri returned.

Well, nothing ventured ever won fair lady. Heart beating twelve to the dozen, I jumped across to the table that held the box of diskettes, flipped the lid up, and picked one out at random. I slipped it into the breast pocket of my shirt, and was sitting in my chair looking harmless when Scheri came back. Maybe I could get my mate Steve to find out what was on the diskette.

Scheri filled the coffee maker and switched it on. Then she sat down and swivelled her chair to face me, giving me the feeling that if I moved my head slightly to the right, I would just about be able to see her breakfast. I fixed my gaze on her big blue eyes. She reached over and put her hand on my arm.

'Kenny, I need a favour. Would you give me a ride home to

get my car? I came in with Quinn this morning, and now he's high-tailed it to Bish ... someplace in Hamp-shire and he won't be back till Friday morning. Would you mind?'

She tilted her head to one side, raised her eyebrows, and gave me what she probably thought was a cute smile. I thought so too.

'Sure thing,' I said, trying to talk American. 'No problem. I've got a couple of cars to deliver around half-past four, but I should be back by five thirty, easy. I'll take you then. OK?'

A cloud dropped on her face and made me feel really sorry for her. She said:

'Gee, that's no good! It has to be soon. There's something I need to pick up at home as well. How about we have our coffee, then I'll lock up the office, and we go?'

Well, how could I refuse? When Scheri and I walked out through the workshop, Peasel shouted:

'Hey, Kenny, you forgot your bike.'

I ignored him, of course. But Jeff's Brummie voice answered.

'Leave it be, lad; he prob'ly wouldn't have the strength to ride it back, anyhow.'

In the car I was conscious of Scheri's perfume. I hoped it wouldn't hang about long enough for Aileen to detect the next time she was in the car. It was perfectly innocent, of course, but Aileen can be pretty unreasonable at times, as you know. When we got to Snitterfield, which is between Stratford and Warwick, Scheri directed me to a bunch of small modern houses grouped around a shared lawn edged with bushes and flower beds. I stopped in the street behind her little red Honda. She said:

'Come on in for a minute,' and without giving me a chance to refuse, she got out and led the way to a bungalow.

Inside, it was quite stylishly furnished. Scheri ushered me on to a sofa, and said:

'Fancy a drink, honey? You'd like a scotch, wouldn't you?'

I said OK, and all at once I remembered I had one of her diskettes nestling in my shirt pocket. I was sure the unmistakable outline of the thing must be visible, and wished I had worn my jacket; though that would have made me uncomfortably hot in this weather.

Scheri brought a generous glass of whisky and put it down on the little table beside the sofa, saying:

'Here you go. Just give me a couple of minutes, and then I'll be right with you.'

She left the room; and I heard water running, while I sipped at the whisky. She hadn't been gone more than five minutes, when she reappeared with a white towel wrapped around her. My hormones were ready to bet she wasn't wearing anything else. As she walked towards me I felt the panic rising. And that wasn't the only thing that was rising either. I tried to think of something to say – something, you know, to change the direction things were taking. The best I could come up with was:

'Maybe I should be getting back. Those parts we ordered might be delivered any time.'

'Loosen up, honey,' she said in a huskier voice than usual. 'Right now, I ain't too interested in car parts – it's your parts I'm after. And you can't fool me into thinking you're not interested. That there bulge in your pants says different.'

She ran a fingernail along it. Just in case I thought she meant some other bulge, I suppose.

Then – oh, my God – she bent over and slowly started to unbutton my shirt. I felt as if the diskette in my pocket had lit up and was shining through the material. Panicking, I ripped open the rest of the buttons before she could get to them. I whipped my shirt off, rolled it up with the pocket on the inside of the bundle, and tossed it to the floor.

She said, 'Hey, that's better. I like enthusiastic co-operation in my men.'

She put an arm round my shoulders. Her other hand went under my knees. She picked me up like I was a child, and carried me into the bedroom without the least sign of effort. When she dumped me down on the bed, I could see that a kind of glazed look had come into her eyes, and just about then her towel fell off. The vision *that* revealed must have made my eyes glaze over as well, and I found myself doing some genuine enthusiastic co-operation as we both struggled to get the rest of my clothes off.

'My God,' she breathed as she straddled me, 'Ah'm as horny as a dog on fire. You wouldn't believe how long it is since I had a really good screw.'

There was no more conversation for a while. The action got

quite frenzied, and for me the whole thing went by in a pink blur – a very pleasant pink blur, as I recall, but a blur all the same. Scheri came like the Dagenham Girl Pipers and I was not far behind though a lot quieter. Afterwards, I was quite out of breath, but I looked up and felt as if I had won the Golden Globe award – twice. Not that I'm complaining, you understand.

'Christ, I needed that,' Scheri murmured sleepily, and snuggled down beside me.

Gradually, my troubles seeped back into my mind. I realised that I had found out something new about Quinn. Was he gay? Or impotent? Or what? Not that it mattered. In fact, it was a pretty useless piece of information. Another thought struck me.

'Scheri,' I said, 'here we are in bed together, and I don't even know your last name. It's not Quinn, is it?'

'No – it's Lamar, the same as our second President.'

'The second President? Was he right after George Washington then?' About the only thing I knew of American history was the name of the first President.

'No, silly!' She was laughing at me. 'Not the USA – Texas. When we beat the shit out of the Mexicans at San Jacinto, Sam Houston became the first President; and the second one was Mirabeau Buonaparte Lamar.'

Who gives a shit, I thought. But I didn't dare say it out loud. Still, it showed what an educated lady she was.

We lay there for a while, recovering. I kissed her and, as I did so, it occurred to me that this was the first time I had taken the initiative with Scheri. Just like the rest of my life, really – I let myself get swept along like a piece of flotsam in the wind, until I'm so far up shit creek that I need to make some superhuman effort to get back on an even keel.

After a while, I kissed her again, on the right nipple this time; and we were off once more. This time I was in the driving seat, so to speak. And you know what? It felt good to be in control for a change. I got the distinct impression that Scheri appreciated it as well.

Alone in my car on the way back to work, I found myself hoping Aileen wouldn't choose that night to come all over amorous, and I wondered what excuse I could use to put her off. Then I caught hold of myself – not as such, of course – and remembered my new approach to life. I shouted it out of the open car window, setting a bunch of sheep galloping across a field on the Welcombe Hills.

'Stop being a wimp, Kenny. You're in charge.'

Anyway, it's not as if Aileen and I were married, as such.

11

That night, I got home before Aileen, and called Steve to see if he was free. Luckily, it turned out that his wife Sheila had left that morning to visit her mother in Newcastle for a few days, so the coast was clear. He said to come on over, and pick up a few cans of lager on the way.

Steve lives south of the river. He's got a detached house in one of the avenues off the Banbury Road, so it would be a nice walk for a summer evening. Besides, I had plenty to think about, and I think better while I'm walking. First I headed towards the town centre and called in at an off-licence in the High Street to get the lager and a bottle of Captain Morgan rum. I can't stand the stuff, but Steve laps it up. I was hoping to catch Aileen leaving the shoe shop; it was just about her stopping time. By the time I turned into Sheep Street, though, Jonathan Phillips' shop was closed with no sign of life. I tried to remember if it was Aileen's night for going to the health food store to stock up on seaweed and yeast pills and suchlike. But then, as I passed Falstaff's wine bar, I happened to glance in the window – and there she was. Sitting at a table for two with a bloke I couldn't quite place at the time, though I realised later that he was Derek Something-or-Other, the shoe shop manager. More stuff to think about. I speeded up and headed across Waterside and Bancroft Gardens. From there I crossed the footbridge and made for Steve's place as fast as I could walk.

Steve had his computer running when I got to his house. We opened a couple of tinnies, and sat down in front of the screen. Steve pushed Scheri's diskette into a slot in the front of the computer and pressed a few keys. I watched the screen as if I knew what was happening. Some words appeared there, and I said:

'That's great – your machine can read it.'

Steve just looked glum and said:

'I don't think it can. That doesn't tell me too much.'

On a closer look, even I could see what he meant. It looked like:

```
Volume in drive A is DEFAULT FUL

Directory of A:\

CC509216 005        1457664        07/21/96        10:43

    1 file(s)            1457664 bytes

                                0 bytes free
```

Well, I cleverly sussed out the American-style date, and the time, but that was it. Surely an expert like Steve could do better.

'I'll try a text editor and see if I can read it, but I'm pretty sure it'll be compressed.'

I nodded encouragement while Steve filled the screen again and again with unreadable junk, mainly consisting of little black rectangles and squiggles. He sighed and brought back the previous screen.

'What backup system does she use?'

I shrugged and must have looked as ignorant as I felt. Steve went on:

'I think it might be the Norton Desktop one; see that numbering . . . and the label . . . some of it looks kind of familiar. Norton Backup is what I use, and it's fairly popular.'

'You mean you can find out what's on it?'

'Sorry, mate,' he replied. 'If I had the whole backup set, I might be able to restore it to my hard disk – but then there could be other obstacles to overcome before we can get at the data.'

An idea was forming in my mind. I asked Steve:

'How quickly could you do it? I mean, would three or four hours be long enough to find out all that's there?'

Steve laughed.

'Not a chance. How many disks are there in the backup set?'

'Seven or eight,' I told him.

'Well, I suppose I could do a DISKCOPY of the whole lot in about twenty minutes. You know . . . make exact copies and then try to crack it using the copies.'

He turned his chair to face me, and looked serious. Unusual, that, for Steve. He said:

'Look, Kenny, I'll help you as much as I can; but there's no way I'm getting into anything criminal. I've got a lot more to lose than you have. If you were to bring me some diskettes to copy, I might stretch a point and help you to find out what data is on them. But that's it. If I was ever asked, I wouldn't have a clue where they came from, and I want everything to do with them out of my possession as soon as possible. OK?'

'OK,' I replied, thinking that he was dead right – I didn't have much to lose; just my life. My idea was to get into the office, somehow, at night, and get the whole set of backup disks for Steve to copy. They would only be missing for an hour or so before I put them back. Nobody would ever know.

In fact, I could do it later on this very night. To Steve, I said:

'Right, let's do it later on this very night. I'll go to the Lone Harp office about midnight, get the disks, and bring them to you. You do your stuff, and then I'll put them back.'

As there was nothing useful that could be done for a few hours, we relaxed for a bit with a few lagers, and in Steve's case, the odd glass of rum. I was careful not to drink much on account of I had things to do, so Steve got most of the booze. We talked about this and that, and old times, and girls we used to know. I can't remember all the details, but Steve talked more and more as the evening wore on. As you know, he gets quite philosophical at times, especially with the help of a few drinks. He finally came up with:

'You know, mos' people don't really think much about the world around them. Here's a f'rinstance. This is a fact that everybody knows. It's a really, really remarkable fact – but I've never in my whole life . . . in my whole life . . . heard anyone remark on it.'

At this point Steve paused and tried to look straight at me, but his eyes kept slipping past my left shoulder. I nodded to help him stay on course. He raised a shaky forefinger roughly in my direction to emphasise his point:

'Male cats can pee backwards.'

I decided it was time for me to go. In any case, there were things I needed to do in preparation for my burgling expedition.

I got back home about eleven, to find that Aileen had gone to bed. At my usual place on the dining-table, there was a plate of something resembling a bird's nest that had been out in a rainstorm. Cold, congealed spag bol. Maybe she was trying to tell me something. Well, that sack of worms would have to wait; I had other things on my mind. As quietly as I could, I changed into my black jeans and sweat shirt and made sure I had all the equipment and tools I would need.

I parked a good distance away and walked up Anthony's Bridge Road. At the back of Lone Harp Auto, I pressed the right sequence of keys on the security pad, and used my key to open the door. I shut it from the inside and switched on the lights in the back half of the empty service bay. Then I took a good long look at the door leading to the office. It would be easy enough to break through the door, using tools from the well-equipped bay; but of course, I didn't want to leave any traces of my entry. Anyway, I don't do breaking and entering; I prefer to enter without breaking.

The lock was quite an expensive model, though not really a highly secure type. After all, the real security was on the door I had come in through. This was nothing I couldn't handle, given time and my set of lock-picking tools.

My skills were a bit rusty, so it took me a good half-hour's careful fiddling before I heard that satisfying click that announces a job well done. I wasted no time looking around, seeing as how I knew exactly what I was after. The light shining through the door from the service bay was enough to let me grab the whole box of diskettes. Within seconds I was outside, breathing heavily and feeling relieved that the first stage of the operation was over.

A few minutes later, I was back at Steve's house with the box of diskettes. I was pleased to see that he didn't seem to have drunk any more since I left. He probably wouldn't have passed a breathalyser test, but was obviously in good enough condition to drive a computer. Steve opened up the box and looked at the disks.

'You've got more than just the backup set here,' he said. 'I've got plenty of spare diskettes, so I'll copy the whole lot.'

'OK, so long as it doesn't take all night,' I said, knowing my nerves would keep twanging like Scheri's accent until I had the stuff safely back in the office.

'Relax,' Steve told me. All very well for him, I thought. He's not being kicked around by a ruthless boss and a gang of gun-toting villains *and* the police. But I sat down and watched, while he got on with it. I thought computers were supposed to be fast, but this process seemed to take for ever, with constant switching of diskettes, and messages on the screen going on about source and target disks. It was almost an hour before Steve leaned back with a sigh and said it was finished and he didn't know about me but he was bloody well going to bed.

Getting the diskettes back to the office was no problem. I had, of course, left the inner door open, so it was the work of a moment to replace the box of disks and get out, making sure that the office door was locked this time. While I was closing the outer door, it occurred to me that there was plenty of night left, and here I was, standing beside the door of Quinn's mysterious antiques store. Not only that, but I was equipped for breaking and entering.

Why not?

The big vehicle door on that part of the building was fastened by thick steel straps which slotted over steel loops that were firmly fixed to the brickwork of the building. The steel pins which had been dropped through the loops to secure the straps were fastened in place by good quality padlocks. No problem, as such. In five minutes I was able to prise the door open enough to slip through – and I was inside.

It was a big space; my little pocket flashlight couldn't reach to the far wall. I was standing in an empty area, big enough for, say, a couple of medium-sized vans. Beyond that there was something a lot bigger. Going closer, I made out a trailer – the kind of trailer you see out on the road as the load-bearing back part of an articulated truck. It usually has a yellow sign on the back, saying LONG VEHICLE. On the trailer was one of those containers that can be lifted straight into the hold of a container ship. These things are forty feet long.

Going round the other side of the trailer, I found myself in what looked like a junk shop. It was a jumble of wooden furniture; all old-fashioned tables, chairs, cabinets, desks, chests, bureaux, and such. I don't know much about antiques – in fact I don't know anything about antiques. But it looked like a load of junk to me.

I took a closer look at some of the stuff. OK, maybe not complete junk, but still nothing I would have in my home. Of course, I prefer nice modern furniture. I'll say this for it though; it was all nice and clean and polished. There were signs of some organisation as well, since every piece of furniture had a new label stuck on it, and every label had a number in black marker. I compared some of the numbers, and found E41, E42, E43, and so on. I guessed this stuff was intended for container E. I wondered if the E meant that this was the fifth shipment.

Looking at the amount of furniture, I decided it would take a lot more than this to fill a forty-foot container. So there must be plenty still to come.

Beside the collection of antique furniture, I found two forklift trucks neatly parked, side by side.

I had seen enough. Hardly any new information though; it just confirmed what I already knew. Still, I was impressed yet again at how efficient and well organised Quinn's business enterprises always were. You may not think that's very remarkable, but I'm telling you, your average criminal's arrangements and organisation are usually completely shambolic. It's only because the police are often just as incompetent that so many villains get away with it. So Quinn had a head start; no wonder he could come back to Europe and muscle in on whatever rackets they were that he had muscled in on.

I left the way I had got in, only stopping to fasten the padlocks and the door exactly the way I had found them.

In the morning, Aileen must have got up at the crack of quarter-past six. She was all dressed and titivated when she woke me at seven thirty. Sitting on the side of the bed, she gave me a firm look, and said:

'It's time you and I had a serious talk.'

Bloody hell! The very words Neil used that night in the Mercedes. I struggled up far enough to look at the radio-alarm on the headboard. Three hours' sleep I'd had. I groaned.

'Christ, Aileen! Not a board meeting at this time in the morning. Can't it wait till tonight? I'll get a Chinese takeaway and we can have a cosy evening watching television . . . or we can go down to the Bell and . . .'

I was desperately trying to think of something that would really please her.

'No board meeting,' she said. 'I just want to warn you that I'm not going to put up with this much longer. I never know where you are, or when you'll be back. You come and go as you please without so much as a word to me. For all I know, you could have been out with a woman last night – I know you weren't on a job. It's getting to be more than flesh and blood can stand.'

I opened my mouth, but that just seemed to be a signal for her to start up again. It's pretty hard to stop Aileen when she gets the baton between her teeth.

'And another thing, Kenny Madigan . . .'

In my head, I heard myself saying, Stop being a wimp, Kenny. You're in charge. I held up my hand in a stop sign in front of Aileen, and jumped firmly into the flood.

'All right, Aileen. I get the message. You're quite right. We do need to have a serious talk. I was definitely not out with another woman last night . . . and Steve will back me up on that. There's been a lot of things happening to me that it's better for you not to know about.'

I softened my tone, because she had stopped speaking; but I kept the stop sign my hand was making.

'Look, Aileen, I don't want to lose you; but you'll just have to trust me for a little while longer. Why don't we meet at lunch time? We can go to the wine bar and have a long talk. Get the whole thing sorted.'

She ignored my suggestion and went straight for Steve. Isn't it funny how women are always suspicious of your friends.

'Yes, I just bet Steve would back you up,' she said. 'He would say you were in . . . Kalamazoo if you asked him to.'

I hopped out of bed and gave her a very persuasive hug.

'Please, Aileen. I'll explain everything. I don't want us to have any secrets from each other.'

I thought that might make her feel kind of guilty on account of Derek Wossname – and it worked, for the time being at least.

'Well, OK,' she said, and managed to produce a thin smile. 'I'll meet you in the wine bar at one o'clock.'

By the time I had showered and shaved, and had my slice of toast and coffee, there was a car tooting outside. It was Sylvia, one of Aileen's workmates who was giving her a lift in to the shoe shop. She kissed me and trotted out. It was just like old times. And I really didn't want to lose Aileen.

About five seconds after the door closed behind Aileen, the phone rang. It was Neil, sounding like a man in a hurry.

'Thought I might just catch you,' he said. 'Look, what time do you stop for lunch?'

'Well, it's pretty flexible,' I replied, 'but – '

He broke in: 'Right, meet me at one o'clock on the dot. Down by the river, behind the Brass Rubbing Centre. The only other people there will be tourists – I don't need to tell you how important it is for both of us not to be clocked by the wrong people.'

I started to protest, but he drove right over me: 'Right! Don't be late. We can feed the ducks. *Ciao.*'

He was gone. *Ciao* indeed! That's the kind of rubbish you get from educated rozzers.

At least I got word to Aileen, so I didn't actually stand her up. But frost was starting to form on the phone when she said:

'Don't concern yourself about me. I'll easily find someone more reliable to have lunch with.'

Yes, probably Derek Something-or-Other, I thought. And then I felt guilty about my little adventure with Scheri. But that was a bluebird. You know what I mean; it was like winning a thousand pounds on the lottery – you get it and spend it, and you don't expect it to happen again. Anyway, it wasn't my fault.

12

Neil was there, down on the river bank, snazzily turned out as usual. He grinned at me, and went on throwing bits of sandwich to a couple of swans.

'What's the panic?' I demanded. 'I was supposed to meet Aileen – and I can't even put the blame on to you, because she doesn't know anything about this business. She'll string me up for this.'

'How is the lovely Aileen?' He turned to face me, adding, 'Sally's going to call her to fix up a foursome sometime next week. Where do you fancy eating?'

I felt as if he was having a game with me. This was somebody I had got to like as a . . . well, not a mate, exactly, but a decent bloke to have a drink and a meal with. My upper lip twitched all by itself, like a snarl, when I said:

'OK, Neil. You didn't make me rush down here for a bit of social chit-chat. What's going on?'

He was facing me now, with a piece of sandwich hanging by his side, in his left hand. Out of the corner of my eye, I saw one of the swans was waddling towards the sandwich, annoyed at the interruption to its lunch. I hoped it was going to snap at his fingers.

He said, 'Look, Kenny, it's for your sake that I asked you to meet me . . .'

He broke off and disappointed me by throwing a piece of bread to the swan before going on:

'. . . I wanted to give you a warning. Remember the London mob I told you about? Well, they've been spotted in Stratford again – two of them at least, but there may be more. Hopper – you remember I told you they call him Posh Perce – and a known associate of his, Lionel Bickerstaff. Hopper's the brains, of course; Bickerstaff's IQ is the same as his shoe size, but he's built like a brick shithouse and he's got a tendency to malice without thought. So watch yourself – you won't be much use to me as an inside man if you get beaten up.'

That news didn't make me feel any more cheerful. I shivered. I realised that my knees were trying to tremble. But I wasn't about to let Neil see how scared I was – and I didn't believe for a minute that Neil was concerned for my safety. Bravely, I said:

'Is that it, then? You could have told me that on the blower instead of doing all this choke and dagger stuff.'

'So I could,' he said, 'but then I wouldn't have been able to show you these snaps from Hopper's family photograph album . . .'

He threw the last bit of sandwich at the nearest swan – quite viciously, I thought – and reached into the inside pocket of his jacket.

'. . . and it's in your best interest to know what these characters look like.'

Of course! I'd clean forgot and almost given myself away. As far as Neil was concerned, I had never met the Boss gang. I looked at the pictures Neil was holding out to me. It was them all right. Posh Perce looked just like the kind of businessmen you see in newspaper photos, handing over enormous cheques to charities. And there was Lionel with a puzzled look – as if someone had just asked him to spell 'cat'. There were just two pictures. I wondered if Perce had found a replacement for poor old vicious Mozzer.

'Where would I expect to see this pair?' I asked, thinking that would be a good place to keep well clear of. Another shiver struck me, and I threw in an extra question:

'Shouldn't you have some of your blokes following these nutters, if they're as dangerous as all that?'

Neil's eyebrows moved about two inches to the north.

'Come on, Kenny,' he said, giving me a pitying look. 'You know perfectly well we haven't got the resources to shadow every villain in town. Anyway, they haven't broken the law here, as far as we know. All I can tell you of their whereabouts is that they have checked into the Shakespeare Hotel.'

I was impressed. I said, 'Christ, they don't believe in living rough, do they?'

'Well, they're more than just simple car thieves.'

Insulting bastard! Neil's eyes were laughing at me, though he didn't smile. He went on:

'Hopper is a successful businessman, and his business is crime.

I bet he charges the hotel bills as a business expense against one of his companies.'

He switched to a more official-sounding tone of voice:

'Right, then. I've given you some useful information. What have you managed to find out for me so far?'

I considered that. When you get down to hard facts, I still knew practically nothing about Quinn's rackets, whatever they were.

'I've checked out the antiques store,' I said brightly. 'It didn't seem too dangerous, what with Quinn being away.' I told him about the container trailer and the rows of labelled furniture. It didn't get him excited, so I told him I might have some solid facts quite soon. I was thinking about the diskettes Steve had copied, but I didn't go into any details.

Neil came back to what I'd said about Quinn being away:

'You should have told me that. That's exactly the kind of information I want from you.'

'So what are you complaining about?' I replied. 'I've just told you.'

'Yes, but . . . oh never mind. Where did he go? How long was he gone?'

'Well, he left on Wednesday, about lunch time, and he was back at the garage on Friday morning – today, first thing.'

'Right! Got that.'

Neil had whipped out a little notebook, and was scribbling in it.

'Now, do you know where he went to?'

'I heard Hampshire mentioned . . . oh yes, and she nearly said the name of wherever it was. It starts with a B.'

'OK,' Neil said. 'But get some more information – try to find out exactly where he goes – and it better be soon. I'll be in touch in couple of days. And if you come through for me, you might just get out of this mess unscathed.'

He nodded and turned to leave. I couldn't resist telling his departing back:

'Mind how you go. Look out for hungry swans.'

He kept walking, though he turned his head back towards me.

'Foxtrot Oscar,' he said – but there was a grin on his face.

Making cheap cracks at Neil didn't help me to feel any better.

In fact, at that moment, I felt more despair than I ever had in my whole life. Unscathed, for Christ's sake! Inside, I was well scathed already. But for all that, the police were probably my least worst enemy. Unlike the Boss mob, and even Quinn, they were probably not capable of killing me.

What with my being surrounded on every side – not to mention above and below – by threats and worse, the surprising thing was that whenever I pushed the whole mess to the back of my mind, all I could think of was how to repair my relationship with Aileen before it fell apart.

The garage was fairly quiet in the afternoon, it being Friday. Quinn was in, so it came as no big surprise to me when I was invited into the office to find him and Scheri sitting behind the desk with their business faces on and the ghetto-box off. I was not surprised to learn that I was being invited to perform another car-nicking job. I grinned and pretended to look eager while digesting the details. Another Jaguar . . . from Henley-in-Arden. A bit close to home, I thought, and said as much to Quinn.

'Look,' he said, half closing his eyes, 'I don't tell you how to hijack the cars. And you don't have the right to criticise my business decisions. I'm strategy – you're tactics. Got it?'

Christ, he was shirty. I wondered if maybe he was constipated. But what did I care? I sneaked a glance at Scheri who rewarded me with something like half a wink. She didn't crack her serious expression into any smile, though. That gave me the idea that these two might have had some kind of disagreement among themselves. Perhaps I could find out from Scheri next time Quinn was out of the way. He was talking again.

'So any time next week is fine by me – just don't foul it up this time.'

I handed back the sheet of car details and watched while he went through the usual circus act of burning it in the waste bin.

I only had two cars to deliver back to their owners that day, so I got home quite early. The first thing I did when I got in was to phone Steve – not expecting any real news as such, just to ask when he thought he would get round to taking a look at the diskettes we had copied. He answered right away.

'Oh, it's you, Kenny. I was just going to give you a call about these diskettes. You got me so interested that I spent half the day at work trying to make sense of them.'

'Any luck?' I asked.

'What do you think?' he replied. Steve always tries to wind me up, but doing it now just showed how unfeeling he was over my predicament. It doesn't matter who they are, other people are always too full of their own little problems to care about mine. I wasn't in the mood for guessing games.

'Come on, Steve, I'm not in the mood for guessing games,' I said.

'OK ... OK – keep your hair on,' he answered. 'I've only cracked the whole can of worms. What do you think of that?'

'Great!' I said. And I suppose I should have felt that it was great, but I got this horrible hollow feeling in my stomach at the thought of finding out things that might be dangerous for me to know. But maybe the hollow feeling was caused by me not having anything to eat all day. I went on:

'How about if I come over to your place tomorrow, and you can tell me all about it?'

'No chance, mate,' Steve replied. 'I'm leaving first thing in the morning to drive up to Sheila's mother's place in Newcastle. I'm staying there overnight and bringing Sheila home on Sunday. So it'll have to be either tonight or next week. Sorry!'

No choice at all for me – I was desperate to know what Steve had discovered. Besides, it occurred to me that his wife Sheila would be back in residence the following week. I didn't need to add to my troubles by facing her accusing stares.

'All right, I'll be there in half an hour,' I said and put the phone down, wondering how much more neglect Aileen would put up with. Anyway, she was late – probably in the wine bar with Derek Something-or-Other gazing into her eyes and exciting her with stories about his adventures in the shoe trade. So I left a note, telling her not to bother doing any dinner for me, and for good measure I added a PS with a row of Xs for kisses. Yeah, I know. Bloody soppy, but women like that kind of stuff.

I was at Steve's place about ten minutes later. He insisted on getting us all settled down with drinks and crisps and such, while I was pawing at the bit, all impatient to find out the dirt on Quinn. Finally he was ready to go. He took a swig of lager from his can, and started.

'We seem to have hit lucky. I was right about the Norton Backup thing. I managed to restore all the files to the hard disk on my computer at work. And then when I looked at the file extensions I recognised them as being mostly Paradox tables. What do you think of that?'

I didn't want to hear all that gobbledegook. I just wanted to know what he had discovered about Quinn. I said:

'Don't give me all that crap. Just tell me what you've discovered about Quinn.'

Steve started to make out like I'd pierced him to the quick, but it was just his way of winding me up a bit more.

'Well, a bit more appreciation would be in order. You don't seem to realise what I'm doing for you. It's a damn good thing I have an office to myself, and a boss who always takes Friday afternoons off. Still, I dont know if the stuff I've found out is going to be an awful lot of use to you ... that'll have to be for you to decide. I think I've sussed out most of what's on the backup disks, though.'

'OK, OK,' I said hastily. 'What's this Parazone thing then?'

'Paradox,' he corrected me. 'It's a well-known database software product, and we have it on our LAN at work. I don't often use it, but I can find my way around it reasonably well.'

He could see me getting impatient again. So he quickly went on:

'What it means as far as you are concerned is that I was able to use it to decipher the backed-up files on those disks we copied.'

'So what did they say?' I leaned forward eagerly.

'Right,' he began. 'The first thing I found out was about the Lone Harp Auto Repair garage. It's a good little business, that. Earning nice profits, and it seems to be very well run.' He picked up some sheets of computer printout from a pile on the floor beside his chair.

'I could have told you that,' I said. 'What did you find out about the antiques side of the business?'

I mean, Lone Harp Auto's accounts would be quite interesting, I suppose, other things being equal. But other things were definitely not equal as far as I was concerned, so it was not in my list of the ten things I most want to know about.

He picked up another batch of printouts and leafed through them a bit before handing them to me.

'I found these tables. What they amount to is lists of the items in each shipment of antiques that they send to America. Very detailed ... and dead boring lists. I mean, who gives a shit whether these manky old tables have got Queen Anne legs or fluted pedestals. In fact, the only interesting information in these lists is the costs and expected sale prices against each of the antiques ... all in both pounds and dollars. Still, I must hand it to your boss – the whole operation seems to be run just as efficiently as the Lone Harp business.'

'There's just one thing wrong with it – a pretty damn big thing, too.'

Steve paused for a moment, and gave me a steady look – you know, as if he suspected me of something he couldn't quite put his finger on. Then he said:

'The weird thing about the antiques export business is that it makes no sense at all, from an economic point of view. I mean it's operating at a loss – Quinn doesn't even recover his costs. Look at this one, for instance. Shipment B, this is – and it doesn't include the cost of shipping, which must be enormous.'

He handed me one of the lists. It looked very like the one I had seen on Scheri's screen. I leafed through it till I got to the last page, where I clocked the huge difference between the cost and sale totals.

'So why does he keep on doing it?' I asked, really talking to myself and not actually expecting an answer, as such. Steve shrugged.

'Beats me,' he said, 'but anyway, I went on and analysed the figures a bit more. I was thinking, maybe he uses all of the Lone Harp profits to finance the export of the antiques. But no, it's not that. He's losing far more than the garage earns ... that's more like a hobby by comparison.'

'So what do you reckon could be going on?' I asked Steve.

'I told you already, Kenny. I haven't got a clue. Are you sure you don't know a lot more than you're letting on? You've always been one for keeping things up your sleeve.'

I shook my head, sadly. Even my friends seemed to be getting ready to desert the sinking ship. I was starting to gather up the lists when Steve asked, 'Are you ready for another can of lager?'

'Bugger the lager,' I replied, continuing my preparations for leaving.

'Relax, mate.' Steve told me, 'I'll get you a lager and then I'll tell you one more funny thing I noticed about these lists.'

While he went to the fridge, I flipped through one of the lists without managing to find anything interesting.

'I give up. What did you find?' I asked, when he got back.

Steve leaned over to look at the sheet in my hand.

'See the items that have an asterisk beside them?'

I nodded. Now that he mentioned it, I saw that a few items were starred, but it seemed to be random. There wasn't any consistent pattern that I could make out.

He went on: 'Right, there's no obvious reason and no particular similarities between the marked pieces. It's got me bamboozled. That asterisk must mean something. When I get a chance, I'll do some more checking with the disks.'

There was nothing more to be said. I finished the lager, picked up the lists in a Tesco bag provided by Steve, and dragged myself off down Banbury Road.

Back home with my bundle of printouts, I found Aileen in bed asleep – or at least pretending to be asleep. Saturday morning would be a time for mending broken bridges and doing my famous grovelling act.

But first I had to put the computer lists in a safe hiding place. The information in them might be dangerous, even if I didn't understand exactly how. Hiding them wasn't as hard as you might think; see, I've got this place where I keep my burgling tools, which I don't often use by the way. The light in the bathroom is one of those fittings that is recessed into the ceiling. You have to take a chair into the bathroom to stand on, of course, but then the light fitting can be removed with just a half-turn of the unit, and it dangles on its wires. That leaves a seven-inch diameter hole through which I can reach into the recess above the ceiling. The space is about six inches high and stretches off in all directions. The printouts went in there rolled up tight and held together by two rubber bands.

If you'd asked me then, I'd have said that I had just about reached my lowest point. There didn't seem to be anything that wasn't going wrong; what with Aileen, and threats from every direction. And whenever I find out anything, it just raises more questions.

13

It was Aileen's turn to get the coveted Saturday off from the shoe shop, so the alarm wasn't set for its usual time. I slipped out of bed at eight o'clock and made two mugs of instant coffee which I carried through to the bedroom. Aileen hadn't moved but I knew she was awake because of the hostility radiating from her back. She can show more expression on her back than most people can put on their faces. Maybe it's the vitamins. I left her coffee on the table at her side of the bed and took mine to the living-room.

After a while I heard the shower and knew I would have to stew for another hour before my loved one would be ready to meet the day. I'm not often right but I was wrong again; it was only ten minutes later that she charged into the living-room in her robe, all screwed up to accuse me of torturing whales and abolishing the ozone layer.

'I don't know if I can put up with your sheganigans much longer, Kendall Madigan – ' she began.

'Shenanigans,' I said. That stopped her in mid-nag.

'What?' She stared at me with a frown on her newly scrubbed face.

'Shenanigans,' I said again. 'You meant to say shenanigans, but you got mixed up and said sheganigans instead.'

Aileen came right up to the sofa where I was sitting, folded her arms and stood in front of me, getting back into her stride, if you know what I mean.

'It's no bloody wonder I'm mixed up ... living with you and your sheg ... your treacherous goings-on. Not that I ever see you – out every night going God knows where and never a word of explanation. We're turning into ships that pass in the night and just wave some flags at each other – and in the day as well.

My mother was dead wrong when she said you seemed like someone who would look after me. *Get your hands off me . . .* you . . . you hornswoggler.'

She twisted away because I had reached out and put my hands on her waist.

'What does that mean – hornswoggler?' I was well amazed at that.

'It means . . . it means . . . I don't know what it means but it's what you are, Kendall Madigan.'

'Oh, that's dead logical, that is,' I said, trying to be sarcastic. That was a mistake because sarcasm never seems to work for me, as you know. So I charged on before Aileen could start up again, with the first thing that came into my head:

'Is that one of Derek Wossname's words then – hornswoggler? You know, your boyfriend in the shoe shop.'

Her face went bright red. I thought, Aha! I've struck a fertile gold mine here.

'Well!' she said, sounding all prim and proper. 'At least *he* knows how to treat a woman. For your information he's very considerate and . . . sensitive and . . . well mannered and . . . and . . .'

'And I suppose he's got a bigger dick than me as well?'

I couldn't resist making it a question. It was a bit of a relief when she said:

'I wouldn't know about that. But I might find out if you don't mend your ways. Now I know how Sleeping Beauty felt – after a hundred years of neglect.'

I decided to be cool and not point out that Sleeping Beauty, being asleep, wouldn't have noticed she was being neglected.

Aileen's battery was starting to run down and for once I spotted the right time to lie down and rub my face in the dirt. I won't bother you with the sickening details of all the grovelling I did, which I faced up to manfully. I followed it up with an offer to take her up to B&Q in the afternoon to choose the shelves she's always wanted me to put up for her books.

'Let's do it tomorrow,' she said. 'I've arranged with Sally for us to go out shopping together this afternoon, for clothes.'

I was happy to agree. And when I reached for her again she didn't twist away. We kissed, and I did some gentle tweaking of her nipples through the thin material of her bathrobe. That never fails to take her mind off everything but sex. So we ended up back in bed until it was almost time for lunch.

See how sensitive and considerate I can be when I put my mind to it.

Aileen's shopping trip with Sally meant that I had the afternoon free. I decided to use it for some snooping on my own account. I was well disgusted that the police couldn't be bothered to keep an eye on Hopper and Lionel. These blokes were known to be vicious criminals after all, and the coppers are there to protect innocent citizens from villains like that. It looked as if I would have to do their job for them – not that Neil was likely to thank me for it, though he would be quick to snatch up any information I might pass on to him.

I wore my casual but smart gear; you know, the slightly baggy chinos in dark blue, with a stripy shirt and my pale blue light-weight jacket from Austin Reed's that I splashed out some of my car-nicking money on. The Shakespeare Hotel was fairly busy with a steady stream of punters going in and out. I took a seat in the lounge adjoining the lobby, where a few people were having coffee, and picked up a *Financial Times* that somebody had abandoned. From behind my newspaper I had a view of the front door and also the door that leads to the car-park at the back of the hotel.

I've read enough books about private detectives to know that surveillance, as they call it, is dead boring. Even so, I was prepared to hang around for most of the afternoon. But as it happened I got lucky and didn't have to suffer much more than half an hour of news stories with exciting headlines like P/E RATIOS SET TO SLIDE EVEN MORE. Perce Hopper came out of the lift – and guess who was with him? No, it wasn't the thug Lionel Bickerstaff; it was none other than Nick Pearson. All that could be seen of me when they passed close to my chair was a big pink newspaper. I heard Nick's usual mindless chatter without being able to make out the words as such; and Hopper was just ignoring him as any sensible person would. But they were definitely going somewhere together.

If they had been going someplace on foot I might have followed, you know, unobtrusive like. However, what happened was, they made straight for the door to the car-park – and I was able to see them getting into a maroon Scorpio, with Perce taking the driving seat. I thought it was probably just as well that I couldn't follow them; it saved me having to decide between that and investigating Perce's hotel room.

Now don't believe any of these detective books or movies where the tough private eye goes into a hotel and asks for Mr Marco Sogliani's room number. If he doesn't get a straight answer, the gumshoe flashes a few twenty-dollar bills and that always works – smooth as California Syrup of Figs. Well, maybe it works in Detroit or Chicago but I've never believed it would work here in England. So I didn't even bother asking.

What I did instead was to nip along the High Street to W. H. Smith's where I bought a pack of five big yellow envelopes for ninety-five pence. In the street I dumped four of the envelopes in a waste bin. Then I sealed the remaining one and carefully printed 'Mr P. Hopper, Shakespeare Hotel' on it. Across the street in the computer shop I knew I would find a bunch of young lads aged between ten and fourteen, hanging around the games software. I picked an honest-looking one at the lower end of the age range, and gave him two pound coins to deliver my envelope to the hotel.

When I strolled into the Shakespeare five minutes later, there was my yellow envelope stuck in a pigeon-hole behind the reception desk. I edged up behind a large American who was complaining about his missing laundry, and that got me close enough to see that the room number on that particular pigeon-hole was 203. Right, getting into any room in this hotel wouldn't be much of a problem. I turned towards the staircase to make my way up to the second floor, and as I did so I saw a familiar shape coming through the revolving front door. Mr Lionel Bickerstaff, the well-known intellectual giant.

I scarpered – out the back way. Well, my time hadn't been completely wasted. I had found out one valuable piece of information. Perce's man on the spot, providing local colour, was good old Nick Pearson. And I now knew Perce's room number, so perhaps I could come back sometime to see if I could find anything interesting in his luggage.

*

Aileen and I spent a pleasant Saturday evening together. It was quite like old times. First we went to the Bell where she gradually relaxed over her two vodka-and-bitter-lemons while I had a couple of pints. After that we went on to the China Garden for a nice leisurely dinner. I was telling her about Angus and Senga and the matchstick model of the Sydney Opera House, when she said:

'Let's invite them over some evening. The poor girl's a long way from home, and she can't have many friends here.'

'OK,' I replied. 'What about tomorrow night, then? I'll get in some booze and crisps and we can have a few drinks. We'll show them that we can be just as cosy and domestic as them any day.'

So that's what we did. I called Angus about lunch time on Sunday and set it up. Then in the afternoon, as you know, we had a heavy date with B&Q to choose Aileen's bookshelves. I felt dead virtuous like. You know, putting myself through the agony of a visit to a DIY superstore. But it was worth it to see Aileen looking so happy. We came away with three matching lengths of pine, all the bits and pieces you need for fixing them to the wall, and an assortment of tools. After that I didn't really feel up to doing the work of putting them up, so I said I needed to study exactly where the shelves would look best, and managed to put off the evil day to some suitable night in midweek.

Angus and Senga's visit turned out to be quite a success, though I definitely would not have enjoyed it if I'd sussed that such a diabolical disaster was waiting just round the corner to cut us off at the pass. But scrub that for now; I'm getting ahead of myself.

They arrived about seven thirty, drinks were dished out – though Senga refused everything but lemonade – and we settled down on the comfortable sofa and chairs. Aileen took Senga under her wing right away. In fact the girls got on like a train on fire. At times like that I get mortified at the way Aileen cross-examines people till she finds out every little bit of information about them. It's almost as bad as when she grills *me*. More interesting though, because she's got no scruples about asking the most hair-raising personal questions. The funny thing is that her victims usually act as if she had every right to poke sticks into their lives. And they tell her everything she wants to know. At the moment, for instance, she was hot on the trail of Angus and Senga's reasons for leaving Glasgow.

'It's a very rough place, Glasgow, isn't it?' she was saying. 'You must have been pleased to get away from it.'

Angus grinned and took a sip of his rum and Coke. Senga's red mop of hair swung from side to side.

'Not at all,' she said. 'Glasgow's brilliant, so it is. You should go there sometime – you would have a great time. Is that no' right, Angus?'

'Aye, that's right, hen. So they would.' Anything Senga said was fine with him.

Aileen tried again: 'Well, I suppose some people up there must have made life pretty tough for you when you got married – you know, it being a mixed marriage and all.'

Angus's teeth were now looking like a snow-white island in a black sea.

'You've got the wrong end o' that stick as well, Aileen lass. In Glasgow, a mixed marriage is when a Rangers supporter and a Celtic supporter get wed. An' we're neither. Ah'll put you out o' your misery. We left because I was gradually getting inveigled into a life of crime, and I wanted to cut myself loose from a certain bunch o' miscreants before it was too late.'

Aileen put on her furrowed brow – and I groaned silently, knowing what was coming. She said it:

'But you're involved in crime here, aren't you?'

I broke it up with offers of fresh drinks. When I turned to Senga, she protested she couldn't manage to drink any more lemonade. I thought she must be avoiding alcohol because she would be driving home. I said:

'I suppose you're avoiding alcohol because you're driving home?'

'No,' she said, blushing slightly, 'I havenae got a licence. It's another reason.'

Angus broke in. 'We're pregnant,' he said, swelling his chest out to about twice its usual size. He turned to Aileen. 'If you've got any ice-cream, I'm sure Senga would appreciate a wee drop. She's got this terrible craving for the stuff.'

So we had a cosy evening chatting about this and that and how Senga and Angus liked living in England. But they kept

103

going back to telling us things about Glasgow and how great it was. For instance we heard about Scotch mutton pies – how you can buy them hot in most pubs, and if you ask for a Mickey Rooney pie, you get one filled with macaroni instead of mutton. They told us that when the police put up traffic cameras to catch speeding drivers, within a week the lens of every camera in Glasgow was plastered with the contents of a well-aimed pie. Sounds better than eating them, I thought – but I didn't dare say it out loud.

I seemed to be surrounded by people who came from such great places that they couldn't stop telling everybody about them. There was Scheri always talking about Texas; and now Angus and Senga praising Glasgow. It makes you wonder how they managed to tear themselves away. I wondered if I would bore people about Stratford-on-Avon if I ever went to live someplace else. Somehow I don't think so.

14

Back at work on Monday, I had a busy morning going out on Ergo, the folding bike, to bring in customers' cars for servicing. Just as well, all things considered, because Quinn was charging around like a blue-arsed fly getting in everybody's way and interfering in what everyone was doing. What made it even worse was that when Quinn was out in the workshop he left the door of his office wide open so he could hear his favourite cowboy music belting out from the ghetto-blaster on his desk. In fact it was a relief whenever one of the mechanics used a power tool. Riding around the local roads on Ergo was miles better than being in there, in spite of choking on the exhaust fumes from lorries and buses.

I hadn't forgotten that I had been allocated a car to nick sometime this week, which meant getting out of Lone Harp Auto in the daytime to suss out the area. But we were so busy that this Monday was looking like a bad time to start that operation. Leave it till tomorrow, I thought – maybe need Wednesday as well; and do the actual job on Thursday night.

When I got in from one of my trips, Scheri emerged out of the back office waving a piece of paper and saying she would like me to check a couple of invoices from suppliers. Quinn was out in the workshop showing Jeff a better way to take a gearbox apart or something. Naturally I went into the office with her but I soon discovered that the invoices were just red herrings. Scheri weakened my knees with her best smile and put a hand lightly on my arm. She said:

'Honey, Ah've been feeling a mite guilty ever since our little get-together ... when you gave me a ride back to Snitterfield. Remember?'

As if I could forget.

'Yes,' I said carefully, the way you would say it to somebody at your front door that you think might be a Jehovah's Witness or a double-glazing salesman.

'Well,' she went on, 'that there ... encounter was not the most civilised thing I ever did. And I would sure like to make it up to you-all. Quinn's fixin' to be away for a few days – he's leaving around lunch time – so it would be real nice if you would come over to my place this very evening ... We can have a little drink and a bite to eat.'

She aimed those fantastic breasts at me and I felt myself wavering. It would be a good chance to get more information, maybe – now that I had a better idea of what questions to ask. I took a deep breath and asked:

'What time?'

'Oh, make it about seven thirty. OK?'

'All right,' I said, feeling a bit breathless. 'See you then.'

As I started to leave the office, Scheri said:

'Hey!'

I stopped walking and turned my head towards her, waiting. There was a wide grin on her face when she said:

'Wasn't it just about the greatest fuck you ever had?'

On my way back to the workshop, I considered that question. Two of the greatest, I decided.

Aileen wasn't too bothered when I told her I had to go out and wouldn't be able to install her pine shelves until Tuesday. She was still happy after our cosy weekend, and was going on about

105

what kinds of vitamin pills she would recommend for Senga during her pregnancy. I said that Quinn wanted my assistance in the office – nothing criminal, I assured her. Probably it was guilt that made me feel more excited than I ever get when I'm preparing to break the law as such. Anyway Aileen never said a word about the fact that I didn't have my working jeans on; she didn't even seem to notice that I was wearing my Austin Reed jacket when I left.

Actually I was feeling quite pleased with myself, considering how much I had found out. Just as good as these private detectives you read about, I thought, and right away I had a rush of confidence to my head. I may even have swaggered a little as I got into my car. Philip Marlowe would never chicken out of interviewing a witness just because there might be some danger of sex.

Kenny Madigan the womanising private eye.

Well, pride comes before the holocaust, as they say.

Scheri had her honey-coloured hair bouncing loose. She was slightly dressed in a very short silky-looking green skirt, fluffy slippers, and a cream halter thing that seemed designed to show off the natural independent suspension of her breasts. We sat at opposite ends of the sofa drinking white wine – she said it was Chardonnay – and did some light chatting. There was soft music coming from a stereo system – Roberta Flack, I think – and I could see that the circular table at the other end of the living-room was set for two with just two chairs facing each other across it. Cooking smells were drifting in through the open kitchen door, and they didn't seem to be advertising pizza or burgers. I said:

'That doesn't smell like pizza or burgers. I thought they were what Americans eat all the time.'

Scheri laughed out loud.

'There's more than just McDonald's, you know. We're having southern-fried catfish . . . only I couldn't find no catfish so it's southern-fried . . . haddock.'

She tried to say haddock in an English accent, but it didn't sound English – just kind of strangulated – like the Queen on a bad day.

'Come on over and we'll get started,' she said.

I hung my jacket on the back of my chair and sat down. It was posher than the Empress of Ranjipoor even if there weren't any potted palms. We had salad first and then the fish with another surprise – no chips, just these things Scheri called home fries, and white gravy. Yes, white gravy! It was a bloody good dinner though, and the ice-cold Chardonnay was in plentiful supply.

During the meal I started what I thought of as my interrogation, but I tried to be, you know, a bit subtle. Quinn first.

'Do you miss Quinn when he's away like this?'

'Do I look like I miss that no-goodnik four-flusher?' She thrust her chest forward and I swear sparks flew from her nipples.

'No ... not at all,' I said hastily. 'It's just that most people jump to the conclusion that you and him are, you know, an item?'

I made it sound like a question.

'Time was,' she said, 'but that was way back ... these days he gets his rocks off on money instead of sex. Come to think of it, Quinn never did get real horny ... not like me. Anyhow, I don't believe he can get it up any more.'

I ignored that last bit, not to mention the jiggling of breasts that went along with it.

'So why do you stick with him, then?'

Scheri tilted her head to one side, as if she was considering that for the first time.

'Partly because I ain't had any real good offers in a while ... and Quinn and I ... we've got some great business stuff going. We've been partners in a few very succesful ... er, business ventures. I guess we're, like, birds of a feather, if you want to put it that way.'

Then she looked straight at me, and I swear there was a tear in her eye when she said:

'No, that's a lie. I'm kidding myself ... if only I *could* get away from that Irish ... but you don't need to hear about my troubles.'

Her eyes went down to concentrate on her plate and there was silence for a while.

When I thought we had been quiet long enough, I took a leaf out of Aileen's book and asked straight out:

'So why does Quinn keep going away? Has he got people working for him somewhere else?'

'Yeah,' she said. 'I guess there's no harm in telling you seeing as you know about the antiques. There's the guy with the truck who moves all the furniture around and brings it to our store behind Lone Harp Auto. Then there's this guy Somerville in some village in Hamp-shire, Bishop's Waltham it's called. He's a cabinet-maker . . . a master craftsman and he does repairs – you know, restoring damaged pieces so good that not even an expert can tell they've been fixed up.'

Something went click in my head just then, so I wasn't really listening when Scheri said:

'Anyhow, that's enough about Quinn. How about some of Mom's apple pie for dessert?'

I was still thinking, so I didn't answer right away. Anyway I don't go much on puddings so I would have refused. But before I got time, something slid along my thigh, and ended up in my lap. Looking down, I saw a bare foot wriggling its toes in my crotch. Very nice toes too, I thought, as I felt them lock on to their target and start to wriggle even more. Scheri was laughing at the expression on my face. I couldn't help it: I began to stroke the leg belonging to the foot that owned the toes.

I don't know what made me do what I did next. It just seemed like the right thing to do at the time. What I did was, I pushed my chair back out of the way and got down on my knees to kiss the leg I was still holding. At this point I looked up the length of that leg and saw the glint of golden bush. It didn't surprise me to find she wasn't wearing knickers, but it did give me the brilliant idea of crawling through under the table, running my tongue all the way up the leg towards the Garden of Eden. When I got there, Scheri tried to help by pushing her chair away from the table with her other leg, but she misjudged something. The chair went over backwards and we landed in a heap of giggles on the carpet.

Somehow or other we became undressed and got each other into Scheri's bed, where we were soon back on track. It was even better than the previous time – and it lasted longer as well. But there's no need for you to get a blow by blow commentary on it.

When we were lying all cosy together in bed waiting for the bell to start the next round, Scheri asked:

'What would you be doing tonight, honey, if you hadn't come here?'

'Oh, this and that,' I said. Then I remembered the pine shelves and added, 'Aileen's trying to get me interested in DIY.'

That got me a blank stare from Scheri.

'DIY?' she said. 'Is that some kind of kinky sex?'

'No.' I answered. 'DIY – you know, Do It Yourself.'

'Oh, it *is* sex, then. Well, you don't have to do it yourself, honey; you can always come to me.'

I laughed. I had never thought of it that way before.

'No, you've got the wrong end of the ... I mean Doing It Yourself is building cupboards, putting up shelves – all that Black and Decker stuff.'

'Oh, I get it. You mean Home Improvements. Well ... what I said still stands ... or it will in a minute – you don't have to do it yourself.'

She used her very talented tongue to demonstrate, which made me feel able to start doing things to her again.

I was dozing off as you do after sex, but Scheri shook me awake and said:

'Hey, honey, I would love for you to stay the whole night but I kinda think it might be better all round if you was to high-tail it out of here before midnight.'

I yawned and sat up. She said:

'I guess we could both use a shower, but these itsy-bitsy British showers can't hardly accommodate a prairie dog, much less the two of us. So you go first, honey, and I'll follow on after.'

But I was starting to have an idea, so I said, 'No, you go first. I'm still recovering.'

Scheri shrugged and stretched and I didn't take my eyes off her while she walked the few steps to the bedroom door. As she opened it, I asked:

'If you and Quinn aren't too close, why are you so anxious for him not to know about you and me ... er ... having it off? Why would he object?'

'Well, you never can tell with Quinn,' she said. 'Just because he doesn't want something, it don't mean he's pleased for somebody else to have it. And he would sure as hell hit the roof if he knew I was screwing the hired help.'

That put me in my place; I shouldn't have asked.

As soon as she had gone, I leapt out of bed and put on my underpants. It was only then when she was out of sight that I managed to start thinking with my head instead of my dick, and I remembered I was supposed to be acting like a private one – dick that is. I waited to hear the shower start before I slipped out of the room. There was only one other bedroom, so it must be Quinn's. When I switched the light on I knew it was his room from the litter of Country and Western music CDs and tapes on the chest of drawers and the table by the window. I definitely wasn't interested in them. Straight to the drawers, I decided. But there was nothing except what you would expect to find in anybody's bedroom; socks, underwear, shirts, sweaters and such. A waste of time so far.

There couldn't be much time left, even though I could still hear the sound of the shower. I swept the room with my eyes and spotted the little cabinet beside the bed. A pair of boots was parked in the open part, but above that there was a small drawer. I eased it open and found – well, nothing really, except a litter of pens, a calculator, nail file and clippers, a bottle of aspirins, and a jumble of paper clips. Dead disappointed I was; I don't know what I expected, but there must be papers somewhere, perhaps documents that could give me useful information. I shut the drawer and picked up the boots in case there was something hidden behind them. Nothing there either. I even shook the boots upside down, just in case. No joy.

When Scheri came back all damp from the shower, she was wrapped in a bath towel, and I was in her bed as if I had never moved. I hopped out, kissed her on the cheek, and padded off to the bathroom.

Standing there under the shower, I felt I was a complete failure as a private eye. Surely Quinn must have left some trace of his criminal activities in the house he lived in. Maybe I should have searched Scheri's bedroom instead. It was then that I happened to look up and saw that the light above the shower was the same type as the one in my own bathroom back at the maisonette. Was it possible? . . . Probably not, but I couldn't leave without trying.

There was a stool in front of the mirror in the bathroom. I took it into the shower stall to stand on. The light fitting twisted off as I knew it would, and I reached into the space above it. Bingo! I found something – a cloth bag closed with a drawstring. It contained a heavy object, and when I opened it enough to peer in, I saw a gun – a black revolver. Having got lucky once, I

110

searched the ceiling recess all round as far as I could reach. There was just one more thing, which turned out to be a leather-covered notebook.

I replaced the light and looked at my booty. Neil couldn't ignore this; he would surely have to use it to incriminate Quinn, and that would get both of them off my back with any luck. Of course, I couldn't walk out of the bathroom carrying this stuff. For one thing, I was naked.

Well, you know how resourceful I can be at times. I had one of my inspirations. I wrapped the gun and notebook in a towel and dropped them out of the bathroom window which had a small opening flap at the top. It was nearly midnight, so nobody would be about behind the bungalow, and I would pick them up later.

Right. All I had to do was get dried and dressed and leave. But there was no towel. Scheri had covered herself with one when she left the bathroom; and I had only thrown the other one out of the window. And I was soaking wet.

Luckily, she was in bed and quite drowsy when I went to the bedroom, so she probably didn't realise my clothes were getting quite sodden as I put them on. I just got out of there as quickly as I could, still dripping, and drove my car down the road.

About a hundred yards away I stopped and walked back to the bungalow. I sneaked round the back to get the articles I had shoved through the bathroom window. I was lucky that the moon was about half full, and that let me see dimly once my eyes got used to being away from the street lights.

The towel had dropped behind a thicket of rose bushes, which was actually quite good from the point of view of nobody spotting it. On the other hand it was pretty bad from the point of view of a person trying to get past a million thorns to reach it. I debated it in my head for a bit and then told myself that the best way would be to crawl along the dirt between the rose bushes, worming my way through till I got to the wall below the bathroom window. Otherwise I would be ripped to shreds.

So that's what I did. Not a problem really. Luckily I had left my jacket in the car, so it was in no danger. But my good River Island shirt that cost me near enough fifty quid – it was already wet from being put on over an undried shower – got caked with mud on the front, and the back of it got snagged a couple of times on thorns that reached down to try and scratch me. Anyway, I got in and got out with the goods – except the towel, which I shook to get rid of the loose dirt before shoving it back in the little window it came out of. God knows what Scheri would think I did with a towel in the bathroom to get it covered with rich peaty soil.

I got back to my car with only one problem left. My soggy shirt. I couldn't put it in the laundry basket to be washed. In fact there wasn't anywhere I could put it at home. In the end, the solution was easy. I whipped the shirt off on my way round to the back of the maisonettes, and dumped it in Miss Downie's wheelie-bin.

Inside, with Aileen asleep in the bedroom, my first priority was to hide the gun in the space above our own bathroom ceiling, beside the computer printouts and my burgling tools.

Out of sight, out of mind, I thought, not wanting to worry about the revolver just yet – nor about what would happen when Quinn came back to find it missing. Though I realised I was taking for granted it was that gun that killed Mozzer.

The notebook, on the other hand, might have something to tell me. It was full of names and addresses written in Quinn's tiny capitals – all over the UK, they were – and nothing to say who these people were or what they did that got them included in Quinn's address book. The first thing I did was, I checked among the Ms. I wasn't there. Then I started at the front and went through all the entries looking for a name I recognised. When I got to H, there it was: 'Hodges, E.', with an address in Leamington Spa. Ernie the fence.

Remembering the cabinet-maker Scheri told me about, I flipped to the Ss. There he was – 'Somerville, William'. And right after him was 'Summerbee, James', whose name had been scored through with a heavy black line.

Another thought. What about that Jaguar I found the necklace in? I looked in Aileen's Reader's Digest book for the name of the alleged owner. And sure enough, there he was in Quinn's address book.

Kenny Madigan the great detective.

It was all coming together, I thought. But what to do next? And there was the problem of Quinn's reaction to the theft of his property. All the same, I *had* to take the notebook and gun once I had found them; to leave them would have been like shooting a gift horse in the foot.

I could see how their disappearance might cause trouble for Scheri. Still, maybe it would break up their business partnership. Just so long as it didn't lead Quinn to me. I would hate to go down the same road as poor old Mozzer.

15

First thing in the morning I called Neil before he left for work. He didn't sound well pleased to hear from me at first, but I said I had something very important to tell him.

'So tell me,' he said.

'No chance, mate,' I replied. 'It's too complicated for the phone ... Besides, there's something I want to get rid of as soon as I can and you'll need to take charge of it.'

Now he was interested.

'OK, do you want to make it lunch time again?'

'No,' I said, feeling that I had the whip hand for once. 'Just be in the Windsor Street multi-storey car-park at eleven o'clock – level 2. Oh, and bring your briefcase.'

'Right,' he said and hung up.

Neil was not much of a one for conversation in the morning, it seemed. I wondered if he was going off Sally at last.

Aileen must have come out of the bathroom while I was on the phone, because when I turned round she was just standing there and I could tell from her eyes that she had heard the conversation.

'That was Neil, wasn't it.'

It wasn't a question. How did she know that, for Christ's sake?

'You're hiding something from me. I have a right to know,' she said. She didn't stamp her foot, but she looked it. I could have toasted muffins on her cheeks.

'Aileen ... I was trying to save you from being worried. I'm going to tell you about it when it's all over.'

If it ever is, I thought, suddenly getting a bubble of hopelessness in my stomach.

113

'Tonight!' she said, not stamping her foot again. 'Tonight you are not going out. You are not putting up the shelves – they can wait. You are going to sit down and tell me what is going on. I deserve some consideration . . . I might even be able to help.'

I nodded. 'OK, tonight then.'

It might even be nice to have somebody in my corner for a change.

On the other hand, as my Auntie Ursula used to say, a trouble shared is a trouble doubled.

I got through my chores at Lone Harp Auto in good time and then told Angus I was going off to start checking out the car I was to nick. It was Tuesday and I had decided to pull the job on Thursday night, so I had to get a move on. But first there was my meeting with Neil. A quick trip into Quinn's empty office to carefully put one of his Country and Western music tape cassettes in a plastic bag; dump Ergo in the boot of my Cavalier and I was ready to go.

There's only one way out of Anthony's Bridge Road if you're leaving the trading estate. It involves a couple of corners to get into Compass Road which connects with the main Alcester road that leads to the rest of the world. I was tootling along this Compass Road when my mirror showed a grey Escort behind me.

Well, I'm not polaroid, so it was just another piece of traffic as far as I was concerned. What made me take notice of it was that when I stopped at the temporary lights just before the main road (there's always somebody digging the road up there), the Escort pulled in to the kerb about fifty yards back. Nobody got out. After I got the green and moved on, I saw that it had come through as well and was still about the same distance behind.

When I turned in at the multi-storey I stopped in the entrance long enough to see the Escort come along, pause, and continue down Windsor Street which is one-way. I caught a glimpse of the driver, who was the only person in the car. I drove right up to the highest level and parked there before taking the stair down to meet Neil.

Level 2 wasn't a random choice. Most of the spaces there are reserved by local firms for the use of their staff, so the cars are usually left for the whole day and there's never anyone about. It can be useful to know things like that when you nick cars for a living.

I knew Neil would be early – and there he was, lurking in the shadows.

'I hope this is going to be worth my while, Kenny,' he said giving me the hard eye. 'I had to shuffle a few schedules around to make this meeting.'

I had no sympathy at all.

'Yeah, life must be tough in the Gestapo,' I replied and ploughed right on: 'Here's a tape cassette with Quinn's prints on it. The plastic should be a good surface for getting them off.'

I handed him the plastic bag. He wasn't impressed. Maybe he just doesn't like Emmy Lou Harris, I thought. But he put it in his pocket anyway.

'So what? I can easily get Quinn's fingerprints if I ever need them.'

'You need them now, to match up with this gun.'

I held up my Tesco bag.

'OK,' Neil said, 'so I could pull him in for possession of a firearm – big deal. I'm already in a position to get him for car theft. You as well, don't forget. No, I need something bigger than that.'

'Would murder be big enough?' I asked.

Now I had him by the curlies. His eyes bulged a bit and I could almost hear him thinking *promotion*.

'Tell me all about it, Kenny.' He was dead friendly now.

I took a deep breath. 'Well,' I began, 'I've got reason to believe that it might have been Quinn who shot Moz . . . er, that mate of Hopper's you told me about – you know, the one whose body was found on the south coast.'

I had definitely cast my bolt now. I had to go on. So I told him where I got the gun – not about Scheri, though. I let him think I had got into the bungalow under my own steam.

Neil was thinking fast now. He put the gun in his briefcase and asked:

'When will Quinn be back?'

'Friday afternoon,' I told him. I knew this from Scheri.

'Right, here's what we have to do,' he said all decisive like: 'I'll take the gun and have it fired so we have a bullet to compare with the one that was taken out of Mostyn at the autopsy. The Bognor police will have that. Then I want this weapon replaced before Quinn gets back, so that he won't be alerted by finding it missing. Oh, and we'll also pick the prints off it and check them against the cassette. How do you feel about putting the gun back where you got it?'

I wasn't wild about the idea – I might really have to break into the bungalow. Luckily, Neil had second thoughts. He was thinking he couldn't necessarily trust me a hundred per cent. He changed it:

'No, scrub that. I'll send a couple of my people to do it. They'll be dressed as telephone engineers, and they'll have whatever keys they need. Above the light in the bathroom, you said? That's a common hiding place; these criminal types have no imagination.'

'Yes,' I replied, deciding I'd better find a different secret nook for myself. 'And this goes beside it. It's just an address book.'

I gave it to him.

'All right,' he said, flicking through it, 'but I'll photocopy it first. I'm going to be too busy for a while to follow up any of these addresses. Maybe later. Well done, Kenny, I knew you would come through with something good.'

Praise from a copper. Suddenly he was every manager I ever worked for, using carrots and sticks to manipulate me.

I said: 'Wait till I've gone before you leave. I think I was followed, so somebody could be watching for me to come out. I wouldn't want to be seen consorting with the filth.'

I was quite pleased with my morning's work. If Quinn was in the frame for murder, the whole thing might be solved without the antiques business and the car racket being blown apart. They could just stop – and maybe no harm would come to me and my friends.

My friends in this case being Angus and Scheri.

It had been my intention to go straight out towards Coventry to survey the area of my car-nicking job. But now I knew – or at least suspected – that somebody was interested in my movements, I changed my mind and went back to Lone Harp Auto, driving very slow. See, I was afraid I might have lost my follower and wanted to give him every chance to pick me up again. Anyway I pottered around the storeroom for half an hour and then decided to set off again.

It worked. Again I was half-way along Compass Road when I noticed the Escort in position behind me. Of course, I didn't make for Coventry. Instead I headed out towards Evesham. There's one of those big country pubs on a fairly main road not far out of the town of Evesham, and that's where I was going. I slowed down in plenty of time, and indicated I was turning in at the Queen's Arms, or whatever it's called.

This place has parking all the way round and several entrances. As it was lunch time, there was a good sprinkling of cars already parked. I found a slot at the front, locked my car, and walked towards the nearest door. As I got there I caught sight of the Escort – out of the corner of my eye, like. It swept in, seemed to hesitate, and vanished round behind the pub.

I went inside and stopped behind the door, looking out through a glass pane. Sure enough, the Escort appeared round the other side and slid into a space only three along from the one I had parked in. Its occupant didn't get out; he seemed to be settling down to keep an eye on my car and the door I went in.

What a bloody amateur!

It was no problem for me to slip through the pub, get out of a back door, and nip carefully round to the front. My friend should be concentrating all his attention in the other direction, I thought. Still, I kept a row of cars between him and me for as long as possible while I worked my way nearer. Finally I just walked up to the Escort, opened the rear door, and was sitting behind him before he knew what had happened.

'Hello, Nick,' I said. 'I think it's time you and I had a little chat.'

He pretended to be amazed. Come to think of it, I suppose he actually was amazed but not exactly the way he was pretending.

'Kenny, my old mate! Fancy seein' you here. Small world, ain't it?'

Being Nick Pearson, he was capable of going on like this for a good half-hour without saying a thing. I was bloody annoyed. I said:

'Shut your fucking mouth and tell me why you're tailing me.'

He nodded his head in that irritating way I told you about

before. His black springy hair went on nodding after his head stopped.

'Right . . .' he said. 'Right . . . Well, you see, I thought you might have clocked me . . . but it's bloody hard following somebody and keeping out of sight at the same time, like – '

I broke in: 'I don't need to know why you were so bloody useless. I want to hear about your new boss from the Smoke.'

'Who?' He tried to look puzzled. 'I don't know what you're talking about.'

I lost my patience with him.

'I'm losing my patience with you,' I said, reaching through the space below the headrest to grab his collar. I pulled it towards me which pinned him tightly to the seat. It was like trying to drag a sack of potatoes through a cat-flap. He spluttered:

'Hey, you're chokin' me . . . All right . . . all right, I'll tell you, I'll tell you.'

I eased the pressure a bit and said:

'OK then, tell me about Hopper and why he's reduced to recruiting losers like you from the bottom of the barrow.'

'It's only temp'ry,' he said. 'See, this Mr Hopper from London had some business up here. He's brought one of his own blokes but he reckoned he was a bit short-handed, like . . . and it turns out he's got a lot of pull with some big-time names in the Midlands . . . and they put him on to me. It's only for local knowledge and this and that – nothing heavy – and he pays bloody well.'

I decided there was something to be said for Nick Pearson's verbal diarrhoea when he started telling stuff I wanted to know about.

I asked, 'So why is he so interested in me?'

'I dunno exactly – but he's really got it in for that boss of yours, Quinn. He reckons Quinn done the dirty on him. Anyway, he set me on to watchin' you when he heard you was getting ready to pull another car job.'

That set me back on my knees. I pulled the collar tighter.

'How would he know when I was planning to nick a car?'

Through his gurgles, Nick Pearson protested:

'Search me, mate – honest. Let me breathe, will you? He must be gettin' inside information or somethink.'

118

There was something in the way he said it that made me pull harder on his collar again. He wheezed:

'OK . . . OK. I was in Hopper's place – '

'You mean his room at the Shakespeare?' I broke in.

'Yeah, somebody came . . . but I never saw who it was 'cos he made me wait in the bathroom. All I know is that it must of been somebody with an injury or somethink. Because when I came out there was a smell of like . . . liniment or somethink. That's all I know . . . honest.'

I decided to give that one some attention later. I didn't think Nick Pearson was deliberately hiding information from me. On the other hand, he wasn't bright enough to realise what else I might be interested in. After all, this is a bloke who thinks Shakespeare wrote *The Pied Piper of Hamlet*. Still, I thought it would be a pity to waste this chance while I had him in my clutches. Racking up my brains, I came up with:

'What about this warehouse in Alcester, then? Tell me what they use that for.'

He tried to shrug his shoulders, but I was holding him too tight. It occurred to me that preventing Nick Pearson nodding his head hadn't made him speechless – that was lucky.

'That's a dangerous thing to talk about for blokes like us who work around here. See, I'm not meant to know this but I got it from hearing Mr Hopper on the phone. It's a place where the big-time operators in Birmingham and Redditch and such store nicked gear from all over; like a wossname – a clearing house, for all the videos and televisions and stereos and mountain bikes and suchlike stuff from around the Midlands. They keep it there while they arrange where it's to go. Somethink like that. Well, this warehouse is quite often empty, so they've let Mr Hopper have the use of it, temp'ry like, while he's in the area.'

Still holding his collar, I leaned over and took the keys out of the Escort's ignition. A tab on the key ring said 'Hertz Rentals'. I let go of him then.

'You're a messy sod,' I said, picking up a fast-food box that had been tossed into the back of the car. It was the kind of white Styrofoam container that you get a takeaway burger in. I went on:

'I'm putting the keys in this box, see. I'll take it to my car. I'm going to drive down that road. About a mile away, I'll drop the box with the keys on the grass verge. So you'll know where to get them, OK? Your Mr Hopper doesn't need to know that you failed the loyalty test.'

'OK,' he said, trying to make up for lost nodding time. Bugger it – I was hoping I had cured him of that.

Down the road a bit, I thought what a good idea it would be to not bother leaving the keys for Nick Pearson. But my trouble is I'm too kind-hearted to do that kind of thing. Anyhow, this way he would just tell Hopper that he'd lost me – not a word about spilling everything he knew. Still, I had a look at the sky, you know, hoping for a heavy shower of rain in the next half-hour.

I carried on with my original plan. Went over to the Coventry area, and started getting familiar with the lie of the land around the car I was scheduled to nick. But I had no enthusiasm any more. My heart just wasn't in it.

I kept thinking about Nick Pearson. I mean, the stuff he told me was far from being high-grade information. Only two bits of it were new. It was obvious now who Hopper's inside man was. Trevor the Germolene Kid was the fly in the ointment which had landed on my menu.

The other bit of new information was about the Alcester warehouse. Dead interesting that, even though it was useless to me in my present situation, as such. Still, when you're dealing with coppers, any bargaining counter is worth keeping up your sleeve.

16

Aileen tried to make me feel at home that night. Of course I *was* at home, but you know what I mean. She produced a dinner fit for a king – so long as the king in question has a local Marks and Spencer branch. There was a bottle of wine on the table as well – the sweet German kind that Aileen likes.

In my head I ran through the list of things which are normally celebrated in our house. Maybe I should have bought a present or at least a card, or something. There's nothing like being accused of forgetting the seventeen-month anniversary of a romantic package holiday on the Costa Brava, for making a bloke feel insecure.

'Hey, it's not my birthday,' I said. 'What are we celebrating?'

'Nothing in particular,' she replied. 'I just want you to know I care, and you can rely on me, and you can tell me anything, and I'll always stand by you and . . .'

I hugged her.

'Thanks, Aileen. You're great! Let's have a nice peaceful dinner. Then afterwards I'll tell you the whole crappy story.'

Aileen served the dinner, and we both sampled it.

'This is really good,' I said. 'What is it?'

'It's from Marks and Spencer's,' she said.

'I know *that*,' I answered, 'I clocked the M&S plastic bag, but I still don't know what I'm eating.'

'It's a frozen dinner-for-two. One of their range of Dishes From The New World. Southern-fried Catfish, it's called. With home-fries and southern gravy. See – it's got white gravy; isn't that weird?'

'Well, it's great. I'm really enjoying it,' I said, thinking it was pretty good but how much better Scheri's was the previous night, even if it was only haddock. I might be getting torn to shreds between Quinn, and Hopper's gangsters, and Aileen, and Scheri, and the law in the shape of Neil – but at least I was eating better than ever.

My Auntie Ursula would have wittered on about a nil wind.

After dinner we sat down together on the sofa and never even thought of switching on the television. I told Aileen all about it. Well, I left out everything that featured Scheri in anything more than a bit-part, of course. For instance, I said I found the gun and address book in Quinn's desk at Lone Harp. And I sort of played down the amount of danger that could be threatened by the Hopper mob.

Oh, and I mentioned about Pudding, and about Mozzer being mysteriously killed, but nothing about his body turning up in the warehouse at Alcester. I told her about all the meetings with Neil; and being followed by Nick Pearson; and checking out the antiques store.

Then I got the lists of antiques out of their hiding place to show her; and I told her about Steve helping out with the diskettes.

Aileen was convinced. 'Oh, Kenny!' she said. 'There was me thinking you were jumping into bed with some scheming floozie, and all this time you've been in such terrible trouble. Not to mention danger. I'm so sorry I misjudged you.'

She hugged me and clung to me. It made me feel like I was a complete rat – and just a bit chuffed at the same time. I was starting to enjoy all that affection when Aileen said:

'Those lists of stuff. I suppose they would be much the same as the other ones that Steve brought round?'

My brain froze solid, but I managed to ask: 'What lists? When? Why didn't he give them to me?'

'Relax, Kenny,' she said. 'It was just the other night when you were out. Steve brought this bundle of computer printouts for you. I shoved them in a drawer and forgot all about them until this minute.'

The first thing I saw, when I got the new lists out of their folder, was another table, just like the lists of furniture with cost and selling prices in both pounds and dollars. But it wasn't furniture – it was jewellery. I ran my eye down the list. There was a diamond and sapphire ring; a natural pearl necklace; a Rolex watch; all small stuff. There was nothing small about the prices against the listed items. The cost prices were mostly in the hundreds of pounds and dollars, whereas the selling prices were all in the thousands.

Another puzzle. What did it mean? And where did Quinn get the stuff? I flipped the list over to Aileen and let her look at it while I got on the phone to Steve like a ton of bricks. Luckily, Steve's wife, Sheila, had a couple of her friends round for a gossip, and he was banished to his little study, so he was able to talk freely.

He told me: 'Remember how we were puzzled about the items with asterisks beside them on the lists of antiques? Well, I couldn't get that out of my mind, so when I got a chance at work, I brought those Paradox tables up on my computer screen. Then I had an inspiration. I tried double-clicking – you know, with the mouse – on the starred items. That generated a whole series of new lists ... one for each of the antiques that has an asterisk beside it. You've now got the full set.'

'Well, thanks, Steve,' I said. 'I only wish I knew what it all means.'

'Don't ask me,' he said. 'I've done what you wanted – cracked the files. A little gratitude wouldn't go amiss.'

By this time, Aileen was right up beside me, trying to hear both ends of the phone conversation.

'But what the hell use is it?' I said.

'I don't know ... maybe your friend the policeman would know. One thing I can tell you from being in the insurance industry; it's amazing how much jewellery ... this kind of stuff ... goes missing. You'd never believe what some people have got stashed away.'

'Yeah, but not somebody like Quinn,' I said.

'Well, perhaps he's got a whole stable of burglars who nick it for him, like you nick cars.'

I perked up and Aileen's head nodded. Steve was doing some creative thinking now, though I could have done without the mention of nicking cars.

'Interesting idea – but, no. It's too ridiculous.' I shook my head. And then I remembered Ernie the Fence in Leamington – and the necklace I found in that Jaguar. I started scraping some more sensible ideas together. 'He wouldn't need his own burglars. The country's full of people robbing on their own account – for pleasure and profit, you might say. It's only the amateurs that try to flog stuff to punters in pubs; professional thieves take their loot to fences and let it go for about a tenth of its real value.'

Steve was making encouraging noises. 'Go on,' he said.

'The question is; how do the fences get rid of the stolen goods?'

'Maybe I can help you there,' he said. 'I shouldn't tell you this, but the big insurance companies have recently formed a joint task force to look into the movement of stolen goods so that they can share information. I've seen some of their reports.'

He paused for a moment, probably to make me more impatient. I waited patiently, not to give him the satisfaction. Eventually he got his wheels back on the road.

'Up to a couple of years ago it was all pretty haphazard and *ad hoc*. Every fence made his own arrangements and lived in fear of stolen goods being traced back to him. Then it all changed. Some well-organised London mob stepped in.

'They buy up the more valuable loot from fences all over the country and use their organisation to move it to a different part of the country, where it hopefully won't be so hot, and can be resold more easily. The fence gets maybe a fifty per cent mark-up and a lot less risk. Oh, and we believe they are trying to set up connections in other countries in Europe – that would make it an even more profitable racket.'

I was with him every step of the way now. Posh Perce's appearance in our neck of the woods couldn't be just a coincidence. I was glad I hadn't told Steve too much about the Boss gang.

I leaned forward, getting excited in spite of myself.

'Suppose someone like Quinn came on the scene with a way of getting stolen jewellery to America?'

'Right!' he said. 'The loot could be unloaded into the legitimate market in the States at something approaching its real value. And that would enable him to pay the fences a higher price than they can get from the British mob. He would only need to offer them two or three times what they paid; and he still gets it for less than a third of its real value. That's brilliant.'

'So it looks as if Quinn is laundering jewellery.'

Steve sounded dead serious then when he said:

'This is as far as I go, Kenny. I don't want to hear any more. We're still mates, but keep your shady lifestyle away from me. OK?'

When Steve got off the line, I sat back. It was all slotting into place. But I still didn't know how he was doing it – not exactly.

'Well,' I said to Aileen, 'we've got plenty food for thought . . . that's about as much as we can handle for one night.'

'Nonsense,' she said. 'We can't stop now. You've got to find out enough so that you can steer your way to safety without anybody else taking a crack at you. I warned you about that Quinn right at the start, but you wouldn't hear a word against him.'

I ignored her revision of the past, and just pointed out that I had only said there was nothing more we could do tonight. But she wasn't ready to shut up yet.

'Look here, Kendall Madigan, we can't let this situation keep drifting on like a Gypsy in the tide. We've got to grab it by the ears and give it a good shake. You're too easy-oasy for your own good, Kenny. You expect to sail through life without any effort.

Well, it's time you got up off your lackadaisical bum and took your own destiny by the horns.'

I was dead miffed at that. It seemed to me like I had done a bloody good job to find out as much as I had. But I kept my mouth shut, waiting for Aileen to realise that she couldn't come up with anything I hadn't thought of already.

'Right,' she said again and went on – talking slower now because she was thinking at the same time. 'Let's leave it alone for now and get an early night. It's an awful lot of stuff for me to digest. But I'll find some way to help you out of your troubles, don't you worry. They're *our* troubles now.'

Getting an early night was Aileen's way of telling me she wanted us to go to bed and have sex until I was too exhausted to move ... and then she would do the moving for both of us until I became a total wreck. So that's what we did.

After Aileen's motor ran down, I was lying there on my side of the bed, letting sleep creep up on me, when her voice jerked me awake.

'Kenny,' she whispered, 'I've been thinking. Shall I tell you now – or do you want to wait till morning?'

I just grunted. She was going to tell me anyway.

'These Hopper people. Why are they here? What are they trying to do? And why were they having you followed? We must try to find out. In fact I'll help you to find out.'

So it was *we* now. But it wasn't *we* that kept having to put our heads in the lion's den – just me.

I left for work the next morning – that was the Wednesday – without being given the benefit of any more of Aileen's pathetic ideas about the Hopper gang. All the same, I should have known that she wouldn't let go. Have I mentioned that she's got a mind like a rottweiler?

It was about half-past ten when Angus came out of the office and told me I had a phone call and it was Aileen. That was so unusual that I thought something must be wrong. But no, it was just Aileen sounding a bit more excited than usual.

'Get round to the Shakespeare as soon as you can and have a look in Hopper's luggage – he's out for the whole day.'

'What do you mean?' I said. 'How do you know that?'

She sounded as if she was losing her patience with me.

'Honestly, Kenny, you're so slow on the uptake sometimes. There's a chance you might find out some useful information . . . an address book or something like that one of Quinn – '

'No, Aileen,' I interrupted. 'I meant how do you know he'll be out all day?'

'Oh, that? I went to the hotel and asked. How do you think I would know?'

I could hardly believe it.

'But they don't hand out information about their guests just like that. And what would you have done if they had called Hopper's room to say that someone was asking for him?'

She had an answer for that too:

'Honestly, Kenny! You just keep thinking up problems. It's perfectly simple. I looked in the car-park – no maroon Scorpio. So it was a safe bet that he was out. And hotels will tell you anything if you ask the right questions. I went to reception and said my boss had sent me round to see if Mr Hopper would be free to have another meeting with him today or tomorrow. Anyway, it turned out that the girl on reception was Sheila Martin. I don't think you know her; she was in my class in school, so there was no problem about getting information.'

'OK, then, tell me exactly what information you got.'

'Mr Hopper and his friend, the tall man in room 204 – that must be the one you called Lionel – they both went out early this morning. Before he went out, he stopped at reception to say they wouldn't be lunching in the restaurant today, on account of they wouldn't be back until six this evening. And he mentioned they would both be checking out tomorrow, probably around midday.'

Aileen paused.

'Isn't that good news? It looks as if they're giving up and going home without causing any more trouble.'

'Yes,' I said, thinking hard, 'that sounds as if it might be good news. Thanks Aileen, you're a treasure.'

Maybe it was good that they were leaving the area. Of course they still had a day and a night and part of another day in which they could cause trouble. At that moment my stomach worked out that there was danger ahead. It suddenly started feeling as if it had been wheel-clamped. My brain cells were slower off the

126

mark, and kept trying to tell me that everything would be all right.

There was no problem about getting away from Lone Harp Auto. As far as anybody there knew, I was still on one of Quinn's little jobs. And I actually was, too. I reckoned I needed one more daytime visit to the home of that BMW.

On my way out, I stopped by the bench where Jeff had a carburettor in pieces.

'That Mr Summerbee you told me about,' I asked him, 'what kind of shop was it that he had in Birmingham?'

Jeff looked round at me as if I was stupid.

'A jeweller's, of course. Everyone knows that.'

I went to the maisonette first to get my lock-picking equipment and a little bag of electrical tools that I keep for special occasions. It's got small screwdrivers, pliers, an ammeter, bits of wire, connectors, and stuff like that. Not that I ever use them as such. Just carrying that kind of bag gives you a passport to any part of public and semi-public buildings, and hardly ever any questions asked. Even better than that is the absolutely true fact that nobody remembers seeing you. It's as if electricians and telephone engineers are invisible.

The back door into the Shakespeare Hotel was open, so I didn't even have to pass the reception desk. I just went straight up the back stairs to the second floor. A maid was picking towels off her trolley outside a room about half-way along the corridor. She didn't look like a girl who would have a degree in nuclear cosmology; more the sort of chick I was used to dealing with, in fact. Quite cute actually.

As I walked slowly towards her, I took a blank piece of paper from my top pocket and pretended to study it. I stopped near the trolley and looked around as if I was lost. I said:

'It says here the master cable can be accessed from room 203. Where would that be?'

The little maid smiled helpfully and pointed farther down the passage.

'About three doors along on the left,' she said.

I lit her up with one of my best smiles; and threw in a wink to go with it.

'Downstairs they told me there would be a gorgeous creature who could let me into the rooms. That must be you.'

'Oh, you lot are terrible. I don't believe a word you say,' she told me, taking a bunch of keys from her apron pocket. She unlocked 203 for me and turned to go back to the trolley, saying:

'My name's Maureen. If you fancy a cup of tea later on, I'll be in the pantry at the top of the main stairs.'

'Thanks,' I said. 'I'm . . . er, Derek. I might just take you up on that offer if they stop rushing me off my feet for five minutes.'

The best way to get somebody on your side is to share a moan about the management, I find. It always works.

I gave Maureen a wave, and went on into Hopper's room.

Right away I recognised something – a yellow envelope lying beside the television with my writing on it. Perce must have been puzzled when he found it was empty. I quickly opened out my tool-bag on the floor and used a screwdriver to remove an electrical power point from the wall. I left it dangling by its wires as camouflage while I checked the room.

All his stuff was good quality; I'll give him that. Whatever rackets he was running, they certainly brought in the money – big time. I went through his leather suitcase – nothing of interest. Then I turned my attention to the wardrobe; a couple of expensive suits with pockets empty except for a couple of credit card receipts for petrol. A pair of black shoes which I shook upside-down and found empty. It was the same story in the drawers where Posh Perce kept his supplies of natty underwear and socks.

Finally I drew another blank in the bedside cabinet that held nothing but a Gideon bible. In desperation I even riffled through the bible in case there was something between the pages, but it looked as if it had never been opened before.

Oh well, at least I tried. Aileen wouldn't be able to say I hadn't followed up her bright idea. Before leaving, I thought I might as well have a look in the bathroom just so I could tell Aileen how thoroughly I had searched the place.

A bloody good thing I did, too. As soon as I opened the bathroom door I saw it. A navy blue toilet bag with the name of a famous Italian designer on it – very posh. Somehow I knew right away that there must be something interesting in it. There was – even though I didn't have a clue about what it was or what it was for.

Or rather they, because there were four of them. See, there was this brown box made of thick cardboard wrapped up in a washcloth. There was no label on the box, but when I took the lid off I saw two little packages each about the size of a bar of soap. That was the top layer – underneath them was another pair. The wrapping was soft greasy paper of the kind you sometimes find around delicate mechanical spare parts. I could see that one had been opened because it had been rewrapped carelessly.

I lifted that one on to the Formica surface and carefully peeled back the paper. The thing inside was a little slab of mostly plastic material with metal tabs attached and what looked like a pair of electrical terminals. I picked it up, using a piece of toilet paper to avoid touching it directly, and looked around for something to put it in. The yellow envelope sprang to mind; after all, I had paid for that. I got it from the bedroom, dropped the gadget inside, and carefully stashed it away in my tool-bag.

It took me about ten minutes to arrange the brown box just the way I had found it, with a carelessly wrapped doodah on top, and the other three looking undisturbed. Except that one of the little packages in the bottom layer now contained a real bar of soap.

I screwed the power point back into place and slipped out of the room, definitely not intending to join Maureen for a cup of tea. I tiptoed past the pantry and down the back stairs without seeing a living person.

I didn't know what I had, but I convinced myself that it was definitely something important. My first port of call was back home to drop off my tool-bag and put the yellow envelope into my secret space above the bathroom ceiling. I still hadn't had time to think of a better stashing place.

After so much excitement, a gentle ride on Ergo around one of Coventry's most expensive suburbs was just what I needed. But I wasn't able to throw off the dread that was living in my stomach.

That night I showed Aileen the gadget I had liberated from Perce Hopper's hotel room – but I didn't let her touch it. Of

129

course she didn't have a clue what it was either. I was beginning to have my suspicions, but I kept them to myself. I just said we should get it to Neil as soon as possible.

We tried to phone him, but there was no reply from his number. The police station operator said he was off duty. Sally's number wasn't answered either, so maybe they were out together. Isn't that just bloody typical; there's never a policeman around when you need one.

17

I kept telling myself that this would be the last car I would nick for Quinn. Surely Neil would get his finger out and stop the whole thing by collaring my boss. Once that happened I hoped I would be able to sneak away unhurt. But somehow I suspected that it would be a diabolical mess and I would get sucked in; it never turns out right for me.

But enough of this whining. On the Wednesday, as you know, I had finished sussing out the required black Beamer to my own satisfaction at least. It wouldn't be a problem, so I decided to pull the job on the Thursday night. As usual, Angus was ready and willing to parachute me into the target area.

After the excitement of the past week, I was hoping to have a nice quiet normal day at work. The late summer weather was warm and sunny, so I quite enjoyed doing the rounds on Ergo. I thought of trying to contact Neil while I was out on one of my trips, but then it occurred to me that that might lead to him forcing me to meet him in the evening. As I was committed to nicking a car that night, it didn't seem like a good idea. I put it off till tomorrow; one more day wouldn't hurt.

About eleven o'clock, I went into the back office for a coffee with Scheri. She seemed more relaxed than usual, I thought, except when she mentioned about Quinn coming back the next day. We checked some invoices and didn't talk about our recent adventures at her place.

I had thought I was fireproof to her charms while we were both at work, but when I got up to leave, she gave my bum a squeeze. That was all – just a quick squeeze and a whispered 'great buns' at the same time. Pretty harmless you might think, but it caused me to have such a raging hard-on that I had to wait in Quinn's office and think about gearboxes for a couple of minutes. Otherwise I would have had to go into the workshop bent double. Why has Aileen never found my instant Action Man button?

So up to lunch time it really was a pleasant day. Quinn was away, Hopper and his henchman seemed to be out of the picture, and my little world was ticking over nicely. Then the peace was shattered by Quinn arriving like a blot from the blue. He came in breathing brimstone and shouting for me. I sighed and joined him in the office, where he was pacing up and down. He fixed his beady eye on me and demanded, 'Where's Mary Arden's Tea Room?'

For a moment I wondered how that could be a trick question, but I knew the answer, so I told him, 'It's in the town centre above a baker's shop.'

'OK!' he said. 'You and me are meetin' your man there in half an hour.'

Not knowing what the hell he was talking about, I changed the subject.

'I thought you weren't coming back till tomorrow.'

That was a mistake. Quinn gave me one of his best glares and stabbed a chubby finger at me.

'Sure I don't need the hired help tellin' me where to be. Just jump when I tell you to jump – and keep your mouth shut till I tell you to open it.'

So I shut my mouth, though I was still wondering who 'your man' could be.

On our way into town in Quinn's car, I gathered that he had somehow received an invitation he couldn't refuse – but that was all I gathered, no details. I showed him the baker's and he waved me ahead, so I led the way up the stairs at the back of the shop.

Mary Arden's Tea Room is in one of those old buildings with beams and uneven floors. I stopped at the top of the stairs and looked around. It's very popular as a place for tourists to have lunch, so all the tables were occupied. I spotted him in a corner, alone at a table for four.

'That's him,' I whispered to Quinn. 'He's the boss of the gang that kidnapped me.'

Hopper looked up from his toasted teacake as we approached.

'Ah, gentlemen, so glad you could make it. Please take a seat.'

We sat down and he said, 'Why don't you both join me in a cup of tea?'

He proceeded to fill two cups from the pot that was on the table. Quinn was silent but was wearing his fiercest glare, while I had on my famous idiot smile which I use when I don't know what the hell is going on. Hopper was immaculate in an extremely expensive-looking suit, white shirt and stylish silk tie. He made me feel shabby in my working jeans.

Hopper looked us over – a superior kind of look which settled on my boss.

'Mr Quinn, isn't it? I'm so pleased to make your acquaintance at last. And you've brought Mr Madigan, whom I have already had the pleasure of meeting.'

'Just Quinn,' Quinn muttered. 'No Mister.'

We sat in silence for a while, Hopper beaming at us like a kind uncle. You could almost hear Quinn seething. I was just a spectator.

Posh Perce buttered another teacake and got down to business.

'You have been causing me a considerable amount of trouble, Mr Quinn. As you are well aware, I have been enjoying something approaching a monopoly at the upper end of the market. So when someone starts poaching my suppliers, I find it deeply distressing – especially since you have ignored my warnings.'

Quinn had himself under control, but knowing him, I could tell that he was almost ready to burst. Hopper's choice of the tea room was brilliant; nobody would dare cause a scene among the lunching tourists and middle-aged waitresses.

'Can't stand the competition, eh?' Quinn was trying to be quiet and discreet but still snarled the words. It was the first time I had seen him in a situation where he did not dominate. Hopper was in control.

'Look, Mr Quinn, I would estimate the current score at one all. I am now prepared to afford you the opportunity of retiring from the fray with your honour intact – and much more.'

Quinn opened his mouth, but before he could speak, Hopper held up a well-manicured hand in a 'just a minute' gesture.

'I haven't finished, Mr Quinn,' he continued, 'you are about to hear something which will be to your advantage. You are clearly a capable and resourceful businessman. I am willing to offer you a share in my business in exchange for your whole-hearted co-operation – and provided that you share with my organisation the technique that enables you to outbid me when purchasing merchandise.'

Quinn hissed, 'What you mean, Hopper, is that you haven't got a clue about how I'm competing the shit out of you. Well, you'll never find out from me. What size of share were you thinking of? I just bet it's less than the hundred per cent I'm gonna end up with by turning down your kind offer.'

'I was intending to allow you a very generous twenty per cent, Mr Quinn. But I can see that your intransigence is insurmount-able. Therefore I shall be forced to wipe your operation off the map.'

I took another sip of tea and waited for the next round, but it never came. Quinn jumped to his feet and walked out without another word. I followed, taking with me the impression that Hopper never really wanted Quinn to take up his offer.

And I couldn't help wondering what Lionel Bickerstaff was doing while his boss was exchanging chit-chat with the opposition.

Quinn sulked in his office for the rest of the afternoon.

When Lone Harp Auto packed up for the day, I drove my own car to the Safeway supermarket car-park where I left it and walked back. Everyone except Angus had gone home. I hung around while he took his time tidying up in the workshop. Then he checked everything was switched off before locking up for the night.

Angus had left his car at home as he usually did when the weather was warm and sunny, so we had a pleasant stroll over the short-cut footpath that took us through the top end of the industrial estate and out on to Birmingham Road. From there it was only a five-minute walk to Angus's house, but Angus made it seem more like an hour by going on about how great it would be to become a father. I mean, I liked him and he was a friend and all, but have you noticed how boring the nicest people can be when they get obsessed about their kids? And this one wasn't even born yet.

Senga had something ready for us – bloody Scotch mutton pies, for Christ's sake, with beans and a pile of toast, and real coffee. I quite enjoyed it once I'd got over looking for things I could throw the pies at. The Eiffel Tower would be favourite, I thought; the Sydney Opera House would be too easy. Anyway, it gave me something to think about while I tried to ignore all the billing and cooing that those two got up to.

Angus was fussing over his precious Senga.

'You're not eating much, hen. You've got to keep up your strength for the sake of the wean.'

'Ach . . . I ate something earlier. I'm not that hungry now,' she said, sounding a bit tired.

'Well, then, what aboot some ice-cream? There's a carton of strawberry ice-cream in the freezer. I'll get it for you.'

'That would be great,' she said, 'but it's not there any more. I finished it off this morning for breakfast.'

Angus looked so disappointed you'd have thought somebody had stolen his matchsticks. He jumped up.

'No problem. Ah'll just nip down to the supermarket and get you some more. It'll not take a minute.'

Nothing could have stopped Angus. He grabbed his bunch of keys off the sideboard and headed for the door. Senga smiled a happy smile at her hero and said, 'See if they've got any pistachio.'

Bloody hell, she even went over to the window so that she could wave to him as he was getting into his car which was parked at the kerb.

Senga's screams merge into the noise of the explosion and the rattling of the windows. She becomes a black outline against the orange ball of fire that used to be Angus's car.

I hold her tight. She would run into the flames otherwise.

I open the front door for Neil once he has picked his way through the mass of cops, firemen, paramedics, and frightened neighbours. He leaves a uniform to guard the door and comes in. He sees Senga on the sofa where she passed out when she couldn't scream any more. He uses his mobile to conjure up a doctor. I stand there numb and feel grateful that somebody is taking charge.

When it's all over – well, it will never be all over, but when things quieten down a bit – the ambulance has gone away with what was left of Angus. Senga has been sedated and taken by a WPC to my place where Aileen will fuss over her and put her to bed in our spare room.

Neil turns to me. He looks grim.

'You're in no condition to answer questions right now. I'll take you home. But we'll have a long session tomorrow. In the meantime you can think about what you're going to tell me – like who would single out a garage mechanic for a brutal murder.'

My brain is running like treacle. Even so, on the way home, it comes to me. Angus isn't the only one singled out. I am meant to be in the car with him – to share in the explosion. I crawl out of Neil's vehicle without another word exchanged between us. Half-way up the stairs to the maisonette my legs turn to water, I have to stop and lean on the wall. For the first time in my life I am pleased to see Miss Downie. She appears and never says a word as she helps me up to my door, where Aileen takes over. And the clouds forming above Stratford-on-Avon are riddled with specks of Angus.

Neil phoned at ten the next morning to say he would be with us in half an hour. It gave Aileen time to bring me back from the warm dark corner I was hiding in. When Neil arrived I was at the table sparring with coffee and toast. Senga was still in a drugged sleep with Aileen refusing to let anyone see her ahead of her own doctor. Outside the sun was shining in a really offensive way, and nobody had told the birds to shut up.

Neil sat down across from me and accepted a mug of coffee from Aileen.

'You'll have to make an official statement later. But for now just tell me about it in your own words.'

I was getting the full copper treatment. Not a word of sympathy as such. I ignored his invitation and said:

'Shouldn't you be out there catching the bastards who blew up my friend – and nearly got me as well?'

He didn't like that. It didn't sound like the Neil I knew, when he snapped:

'What the fucking hell do you think I've been doing all night while you were tucked up in your pit?'

Now I noticed that he wasn't his usual dapper self. In fact he was quite crumpled and short of a shave.

'OK . . . OK,' I said, 'but you haven't just had a lucky escape from being spread around Warwickshire.'

I gave him the bare facts. No frills.

'Right,' he said, 'I presume you were going out on one of your little car-stealing errands?'

He knew bloody well I was. I didn't answer. Instead I asked what he had found out during his night's work.

'A couple of the neighbours saw a mechanic working on your mate's car. They just thought he had been sent up from the garage to fix it, or get it started or something.'

'Why would they think that?' I asked.

'Well, he was wearing a brown overall with Lone Harp Auto printed on the back, so it was a reasonable assumption.'

I said, 'Well, Senga would have spoken to him, surely? She might even have known that he didn't work at Lone Harp.'

Neil gave me one of his funny looks. He said:

'Maybe he does work there. Anyway, Mrs Costello was out. She doesn't drive, so she took the local bus. A neighbour who was on the same bus saw her get off at the supermarket.'

He paused.

'Have you got a brown overall with Lone Harp Auto on the back, Kenny?'

What a sad man, I thought. I hadn't the energy to be offended. I said:

'Didn't you get a description from your witnesses?'

Neil shrugged.

'You know what people are like. They see a uniform. They don't notice the person inside it.'

I pointed out something that should have been obvious to any copper worth his hay.

'A bloke would have to be pretty bloody stupid to wear a calling card on his back when he goes to plant a car bomb. It can't be too hard to get hold of a Lone Harp overall.'

He nodded. 'True; but we've still got to get statements from all the employees just in case. One of them might remember losing an overall; or maybe sold one to a bloke in a pub. Who knows?'

I was pretty sure I knew. I was willing to bet that the Germolene Kid, Trevor, had delivered the overall to the Horrible Hopper at the Shakespeare Hotel that time Nick Pearson was banished to the bathroom. As far as I knew, the only other thing Hopper got from Trevor was information – which was more likely to be passed on over the phone. Still, I did wonder why I hadn't found the overall when I searched Hopper's hotel room. But it would have been in Lionel's room probably, as he was more likely to be the one who would be wearing it.

I toyed with the idea of telling this to Neil. But then I decided it was such a long story, what with having to go into all the stuff about being followed and catching Nick Pearson and all. Besides, what was the point of nibbling round the edge when I could take Neil straight to the answer he needed? I would tell him about the overall later. I heaved myself up from the table.

'I've got something to show you,' I said.

I took a chair into the bathroom and locked the door. When I came out, Aileen was refilling the coffee mugs. She had been listening quietly through the open door of the kitchenette. I handed the yellow envelope to Neil.

'I think I know what this is now,' I told him. 'It was in a brown cardboard box with three others the same.'

Neil opened the flap of the envelope and shook the gadget on to the table, being careful not to touch it.

'Where did you get this?' he demanded. 'It's a blasting cap – a detonator. Demolition companies use these by the dozen to set off the charges when they bring down those crappy blocks of flats that were built in the '60s.'

It was the first time I had ever seen Neil looking excited. I told him where it came from. It got me a grilling that Aileen would have been proud of. He made me describe everything I could remember about my search of Posh Perce's hotel room. And then I had to go over it all again – and again. I held nothing back, except Aileen's involvement, of course.

'You did well there, Kenny. With any luck, Hopper hasn't realised there's one missing,' he said finally. I didn't say anything but I thought that if only Aileen and I had been more determined about getting in touch with Neil on Wednesday night, Angus might still be alive.

He interrupted my thoughts.

'It's a fair bet that Hopper's prints are on this, and probably Bickerstaff's as well. And if the Forensic boys can establish that a similar type was used to set off the explosive that blew up your friend . . . but there's a snag. As things are, I can't use this device as evidence, considering how it was obtained.'

Neil raised his eyebrows and looked down his nose at me the way my high school headmaster used to eye a class when he was looking for a scapegoat. He went on:

'Of course, I could arrest you, make your statement official, and persuade you to testify as to how you acquired this explosive device. A minor burglary rap would be easier on you than getting put away for multiple car thefts.'

'You can stuff that,' I said. 'I've handed the whole bleeding case to you on a plate. It's up to you to find a way to use that thing that doesn't involve me as such.'

I was really pissed off. And bloody aggrieviated as well.

He nodded, thinking some more.

'Yes, well, I must admit, evidence does lose credibility when it comes from a self-confessed criminal, and even more so when it's obtained in the course of a criminal act. There must be a better way.'

'Why don't you have the detonator found in the hotel room where it must have been left by the previous occupant? Hopper was leaving yesterday. The room might still be empty. If the maid found something like this, she would take it to the manager, and if he thought it was suspicious he might call the rozzers.'

I could almost hear the wheels whirring in Neil's head. He said:

'You have a devious mind, Kenny. Have you ever thought about joining the police force? Anyway, what you suggest would amount to planting evidence.'

He was quiet for a minute or two, arguing himself into it.

'On the other hand, this would just be a matter of putting evidence back in its proper place. Can I use your phone? What was that room number?'

I listened to Neil use his official voice to find out that room 203 was still unoccupied. He spoke vaguely about an anonymous tip-off and asked the hotel manager to keep everyone out of it until he got there. When he put the phone down, he turned to me and said:

'It'll be better if I go there with a constable and we search the room with the manager present as a witness. I guarantee that we'll find this detonator.'

I felt slightly better knowing that he was taking some positive action. Then I remembered the last time I had provided him with evidence – Quinn's gun and address book. That seemed like years ago, but was actually only three days.

'What about the gun I gave you? Any news? If Quinn did use it to shoot one of Hopper's goons, that gives them a reason to strike back at some of Quinn's people.'

'Er . . . yes,' he said. 'We lifted Quinn's prints from the cassette case and the gun. I had the gun fired, and the spent rounds have gone off for comparison with the one that killed Mostyn. So we're waiting to hear from Forensic. But that's liable to take a week or two – they have a heavy workload.'

Something in Neil's tone made me suspicious. I asked him straight out:

'What about the gun – you put it back in Quinn's bungalow . . . and the notebook as well . . . didn't you? Like you said you would.'

He looked kind of sheepish and said:

'Well, not exactly. You have to look at it from our point of view – it would be irresponsible to return a revolver to a murder suspect, especially now that he's had further provocation. Anyway, it's better if Forensic have the gun that fired the bullets.'

It just showed how much trust you can have in the police. But I didn't see what else I could have done. Neil rushed away soon after that. At least he had something constructive to get on with.

Senga's doctor arrived at last, and gave her a supply of sedatives. She got out of bed soon after that, and mooned around the place in a dream. Her mother was on the way down from Glasgow to take care of her for a while. In the afternoon I went to Birmingham to fetch Senga's mother from the station. I was grateful to have something to do.

Later I delivered both of them back to Senga's house, where I was relieved to see no trace of Angus's wrecked car. The last thing Senga said as I was leaving was a defiant:

'See that Sydney Opera House? I'm gonny finish that for Angus.'

18

The weekend following the murder of Angus was the worst of my whole life. I can hardly remember anything about it. When Monday morning came it was almost a relief to be going back to work; and yet it filled me with dread. It was dead straight-forward for Aileen, going out to sell shoes. But in my case it was Lone Harp Auto with no Angus. I was feeling pretty low, and the thought of having to meet Quinn made me even lower – not to mention Scheri.

As it happened, Quinn was quite subdued, just like everybody else. He didn't even play any of his Country and Western music; just took charge of the workshop without shouting the odds at anyone. After I had done my car collecting for the two local customers who had booked our pick-up service, he called me into the office.

'Tough break for poor old Angus,' he said, all serious. I could have screamed that it was his fault and if he hadn't shot Mozzer, the Hopper mob wouldn't have blown up Angus and Angus's car and nearly me as well. But I never said a word. Quinn went on:

'Not only that. It's made the devil of a mess of my operation. For all kinds of reasons I'm suspending the car-nicking side of the business – and as of right now I don't know if it'll ever get back on its feet again.'

I should have known. Quinn didn't give a flying fuck about Angus. He was only worried about the inconvenience it caused for him. It sounded to me as if he was working up to telling me I was out of a job. Well, that would be a relief.

'So you won't be needing me any more?' I said.

His eyebrows shot up in surprise. He said:

'Now, hold on to your britches just a minute. What I'm telling you is that I need you more than ever. I'm wanting you to take over as foreman here. Lone Harp Auto isn't going to go under as long as I can help it. It's a really good business.'

That left me scrabbling for something to say. I came up with:

'You could run this place yourself, couldn't you?'

'Yep,' he said, giving me a straight answer for once, 'but there's other demands on my time that prevent me giving it the attention it needs. For example, I've a shipment of antiques to finish packing into its container and get shipped out.'

Quinn twiddled his moustache and gave me one of his low-eyebrow looks. He went on:

'There's another thing. Some bastard's been poking his goddam snout into my private stuff, and something's turned up missing. I might need to chase up on that.'

Christ, I thought, I'm the bastard that took his gun. I spared a moment to curse Neil for not keeping his promise to return the weapon. I felt as if Quinn could see right through me. But I decided it was just my guilty conscience making me feel like that. Quinn was still talking.

'Anyhow, me and Scheri, we both agreed that you're the ideal replacement for Angus. I think she's taken a shine to you.'

Just then Scheri came in. I suppose she must have been listening behind the door of the inner office.

'Hi, Momma,' Quinn said. 'I've just been telling Kenny-boy how tickled pink you would be to have him running the workshop side of the Lone Harp show.'

From behind Quinn, Scheri didn't smile but she blew me a wink that would have caused a hard-on on a dead cat.

'Sure thing,' she said. She was dressed in a very modest way for her, in jeans and sweater and no make-up, but she couldn't stop her figure sending out bedtime signals. Or maybe that was just with me being, you know, on friendly terms with these bits and pieces of hers.

A lot of things were revolving around my brain. My first idea was to tell Quinn to stuff the foreman's job. I thought about Angus and the Hopper mob and the furniture scam and Quinn's gun and everything that had happened. My brain cells held a quick referendum and told me not to chicken out at this stage.

'All right,' I said, 'just until you can find somebody to take the job permanent, like.'

They both beamed with what looked like pleasure, so I couldn't help trying to make them feel as miserable as I was. I asked:

'What did the police say to you? I suppose you must have been interviewed.'

Quinn snapped, 'Just about what you would expect from the pigs anywhere. They always act as if you've shot the President.'

Scheri changed the subject.

'Nice to have you on the management team, honey. I'll bring you up to speed on the paperwork when you get a slack time in the workshop. Just holler when you need help.'

Quinn threw me a bunch of keys.

'You are now responsible for the workshop and stores. Keep the guys hard at it and open the place up before they get here every morning. I'll be looking for routine progress reports. No problem for you, Kenny.'

On the surface he was all friendly, but just below that, something had changed. I felt it in the way Quinn looked at me. I couldn't put my finger on it, though I could tell he was no fan of mine any more – if he ever was.

Running the workshop was hard work – not my favourite kind of thing at all. But it took my mind off things. My first problem came up when we realised Trevor was not coming back. Nobody saw him after Angus's car was blown up, so we were pretty short-handed for a couple of days. Then I remembered a bloke I used to know, Brian Miller, who was a reasonable mechanic and not currently in employment. So I tracked him down and brought him in to replace Trevor. Peasel got landed with my old job of collection and delivery as well as doing normal servicing for the rest of the day. Quinn just agreed to anything I suggested.

So I was doing quite well, I thought, towards the end of that week, and I would actually have quite enjoyed my temporary promotion if it hadn't been for the circumstances and the wasps' nest in my guts.

Everything went quiet too, on the crime front. It was as if the murder of Angus had put the mockers on that kind of activity. I couldn't get any information out of Neil when I spoke to him after the funeral. He just said that inquiries were proceeding and no, he hadn't got any news back from Forensic yet. Just choked me off in fact.

Oh yes, the funeral. It was a cremation. Better than a cold grave in a field of death – but not much better. It wasn't a sell-out; there was just Senga and her mother, Aileen and me, Quinn and Scheri, the guys from Lone Harp Auto which closed for the afternoon – and a police presence in the shape of Neil. It was on the Friday on account of having to be delayed till after the coroner's show. I had to slip out of work to go to that as a witness but it only took about half an hour. Person or persons unknown was all it came up with. About what you would expect.

By the Wednesday night I felt like getting pissed. I don't mean just tiddly and happy – I needed to get smashed, rat-arsed, falling-down drunk. What I once heard Angus describe as mirauc'lous. And I didn't want to do it alone. This looked like a job for my mate Steve. It turned out he was free, his wife Sheila safely bound for the badminton club, so we arranged to meet in the Bell.

When Steve came in, I was exploring the bottom of my second pint. I got another two from the bar along with a double rum and Coke for him. Then we melted into a quiet corner. Of course, Steve was dead keen to hear about the explosion and everything, though he tried to be cool about it. I filled him in on all that had been happening, which took quite a long time, and I suppose it must have got a bit hard to follow as I slid down the slope of the alcohol pit.

Steve was amused at the way my liquid intake made me keep having to go for a pee. Not liking beer himself, he suggested I would get more benefit from it if I just carried my pint mug out to the loo and poured it down the urinal. He said it would cut out the middleman. I ask you; this is a bloke who can swill down Coca Cola all night as long as it's flavoured with a teaspoonful of rum in each glass. Anyway, I got the feeling he was avoiding drinking too much so that he could act as nursemaid to me.

The other thing Steve kept bringing up was these damned lists of furniture and jewellery. He seemed to think that they were somehow central to the whole pitiful mess. Pivotal was the word he used. I knew what he was getting at. I didn't need to hear him lecturing me, saying I should have followed up that stuff about the antiques instead of my so-called investigations of the Hopper mob. Not that it would have made any difference; besides, it was too late now. I told him that.

'Well, it's too late now,' I said, pronouncing the words very carefully to be sure of getting them right. Then I assembled another good sentence in my head and part of it came out the way I intended:

'We jus' need to wait for the Gestapo to get their fingers out ... and ... and then they'll drop on Quinn like a ... a ... white tornado or something.'

I looked Steve straight in the eye to show how hard I meant it, but he wouldn't stop swaying from side to side.

'... an' poor ol' Scheri as well, like as not,' I added, getting this vision of me helicopting her away to safety through a hail of bullets like in a James Bond film. I took a long swig to wash that dream away.

'Scheri? What about her?' Steve asked.

Without any warning I felt tears coming to my eyes. Out of the blue – into the blue. I tried to keep my voice straight:

'They'll drop a white torna ... torn ... wossname on her as well.'

The next thing I noticed was Steve helping me to stand up. Not that I had fallen down, of course. We had been seated at a table, like I said. He must have piloted me home, but the next bit I remember is when he handed me over to Aileen. I could hear Steve's voice saying:

'It's still not too late.'

I looked all round the room searching for Steve, and finally located him standing beside me.

'What?' I asked.

'You said it's too late now – to chase up the antiques. Well, it isn't too late. I reckon it's your only way out of the mess you're in.'

Steve must have left after that. Aileen poured me into bed, and I wish I could say I woke up refreshed in the morning, but it would not be true. I won't trouble you with a list of the components of my hangover. Enough to say that it was a beauty.

It was a great big bouncing hangover with a heavy metal band doing a private off-key gig just for my brain cells.

Kenny Madigan the hangover king of Stratford-on-Avon.

It took till lunch time before I felt like applying for membership of the human race, and that was only with the help of several Alka Seltzers and three mugs of Scheri's coffee. The blokes in the workshop were getting on with servicing cars – all routine stuff, so I just drifted around a bit in the morning. I discovered how easy it is pretending to be busy when you're the boss.

Anyway, it was during my well-deserved suffering that I got to thinking about Steve's remark; you know – when he told me it wasn't too late to chase up the antiques thing. I had to admit it was true. I didn't understand what had stopped me doing more about it. Now that I knew where to find Quinn's master cabinet-maker, would it be worth a trip to Hampshire to see what kind of place this William Somerville had? All that thinking was making my head hurt, so I put it aside for later consideration.

The other thing that happened at lunch time was the arrival of Quinn. By then I was almost well enough to face up to the Tammy Wynette blitz which was going on in his office when he yelled for a progress report. Mercifully, he turned the volume down once I was in and the door closed.

It turned out that Quinn wasn't really interested in my progress report on the day's car servicing. He actually wanted me to agree to work overtime, giving him a helping hand with his antiques operation. There it was – on a plate. Not for the first time it seemed as if everyone around me was getting together to force me into something I dearly wanted to keep out of. I shrugged and said OK, the extra money will come in handy.

'Right,' he said, 'there's another load of furniture I have to get brought in over the next couple of days or so. Once the whole lot's assembled, you and me can get it labelled and loaded. It has to get packed into one of those big containers ready for shipping out to Dallas.'

'Have you got the container already?' I asked as if I didn't know. 'Do we have to take it to a seaport somewhere?'

'No, all these arrangements are already nailed down. The container is sitting on a flatbed trailer out in the warehouse. When we get it packed – and Scheri prints out the documentation from the computer – then I'll call the shipping company. They'll send a tractor – a rig that hooks up to the trailer – to haul it to Liverpool. The container goes on to the next available freighter and gets to ... oh, probably Galveston in maybe four or five weeks.'

'So when will you need me?' I asked.

'I'll let you know ... I have to be away this weekend, so it could be next week. I would think we can get the whole shebang done with three nights' hard work. You'll get paid double time for night work and we can still be home in time for some pussy and half a night's sleep. Right?'

'Right,' I agreed, and got back to supervising the workshop. It might be messy and oily and smelly in there, but it smelt a damn sight cleaner than Quinn's other business ventures.

19

Weekend again, and neither Aileen nor I felt up to doing any of the usual Saturday things. Aileen had wangled the day off (there was some advantage in being well in with the shoe shop manager). She spent most of it with Senga, just to be with her for support and comfort. I went in to Lone Harp Auto for a couple of hours in the morning to tidy up in the workshop, organise last week's paperwork a little, and generally make sure the decks were clear ready for Monday. Angus used to do that. Of course, for me it was only something to keep myself and my mind occupied, in case you think I was in danger of not taking a pinch of salt with my management role.

In the afternoon, I sat in a fuzzy stupor in front of the television with the sound off, occasionally trying to raise some interest in swimming, skating, snooker, rugby league, golf, and twenty-three other pointless ways of showing off useless skills.

When Aileen came home we sent out for pizzas and munched our way through them at the dining-table without saying much to each other. No point in switching on the television, it being Saturday night. I tried some sparkling conversation.

'So how is Senga bearing up?'

'Well, the doctor has still got her drugged, but I'm sure she'll pull through all right. She's quite a tough little cookie – and she's got the baby to look forward to. Agnes – her mother – is staying on for another two weeks. When she goes home I'll spend more time with Senga. Listen, I've been thinking about these antiques and the lists and everything.'

'What?' I said, left in the dust by her sudden change of subject. 'What about them?'

'Steve was right. You've never even tried to find out any more information about Quinn's antiques exporting business. There you were, giving yourself airs and acting like some private eye on television – and you haven't even followed up the most obvious lead. You're all talk, Kenny Madigan.'

Aileen takes my breath away sometimes, the way she can turn everything round to be my fault.

'Look, Aileen,' I pleaded, 'there's nothing I can do as such.'

She stood up. 'Come on. We'll have a board meeting – unless you would rather get to work on putting up those shelves. You've just left them lying there for weeks now.'

The shelves had only been there for one week – or was it two? I decided to humour her. So I sat back down at the dining-table and cleared the dishes to one side. Aileen got out Steve's computer printouts of the antique furniture and started leafing through them. She asked:

'Is any of this stuff likely to be still in the store behind Lone Harp Auto?'

I fingered through the pile of paper till I found what I was looking for.

'Yeah, this one here. Look, everything on it is numbered. And all the numbers have an E in front of them. All the labels I saw in the store had E numbers. I suppose that means they're going in container E. I think this is the one that Quinn wants me to help him pack next week. See, this list is shorter than the others because there's still a lot of items that haven't arrived yet. I reckon Scheri doesn't record things in the computer until they arrive in the warehouse.'

'Right,' she said, getting on my nerves again. Aileen thinks that saying Right all the time is a sign of efficiency. And she was playing for thinking time as well.

'OK,' she said for the same purpose. 'Here's what you have to

147

do. Go down there, go into the warehouse, and get one of these ... these pieces of furniture. Find one that's got a star beside it on the list ... let me see ... yes, that one there ... "E26 Farmhouse Kitchen Chair". That'll be just like a dining-chair – you should be able to fit it into the back of your car. Bring it back here and we'll suss out its secret.'

I should have known this would happen. Trying to share my troubles had caused an increase of one in the crowd of people who thought they could go around telling me what to do. No, on second thoughts, that's not fair to Aileen – she tells me what to do anyway. I suppose she's one of nature's bosses. I sighed and said OK.

When it was properly dark I set off all kitted out with my lock-picking tools and a decent flashlight for a change – the kind you can set down on a level surface or hang from a convenient hook while you work. I parked round the back of the Lone Harp building, near the big double doors of the antiques store. It was pretty safe, I thought. Quinn wouldn't have anybody working on Saturday night to deliver antiques, and I knew he himself had gone away for the weekend, so there was no chance of finding activity there. Still, I didn't feel safe enough to risk switching on the lights; there were skylights in the sloping roof. I got in the same way as before and flashed my light around.

More furniture had arrived since my last visit. The new stuff was in a separate group and didn't have numbers yet. I supposed that meant it also wasn't on a list in Scheri's computer.

Anyway, my business was with the older bunch – the ones with the labels. All I had to do was find a chair labelled E26 and get out. I could bring it back once Aileen had satisfied her nosiness. No, let's face it; I was every bit as curious – and I had my own ideas about how the trick was being worked, as you know.

Even with a decent flashlight, it wasn't easy searching through the jumble of furniture. After a while I decided that particular chair was missing. If only I had thought of bringing the list I could have picked something else that had an asterisk – but Aileen was sitting at home clutching that list in her hot little hand. Another check through the numbers on the items took me crawling over tables and desks once again, and told me that the numbers started at E32.

I flew the flashlight around at random, wondering what to do next. The beam naturally fell on the biggest thing in the place – the forty-foot container that the antiques would be packed inside. I realised I'd never thought of looking inside it. So I went up the trailer's ramp and into the container which looked empty at first, but right down at the far end I found the missing items. They were piled right up to the ceiling and so tightly packed in that they only took up about the front six feet of the container's length.

I could see that when it was full it would be a hell of a job to examine the contents in detail. The Customs and Excise could never check every one of the thousands of containers that leave the country every day. Anyway, they must spend most of their time looking at stuff *arriving* in the UK. After emptying one of Quinn's containers at the request of the police, without even knowing what they were looking for, I bet they would refuse to do it again without solid evidence.

Well, E26 had to be in there. I found it eventually. Fortunately lighter items like chairs were at the top, so I didn't have to move everything. The worst part was putting the stuff back so that it would look as if nothing had been disturbed. It struck me that it might actually be better this way because I could probably get away with not bothering to put the chair back. What a pity it wasn't the kind of gear I would care to have in the maisonette.

It was quite a bulky sort of chair all the same, and heavier than I expected. I carried it down the ramp and headed for the door. By the time I had stuffed it into the back of my car – not an easy job – I was well knackered, I can tell you.

Back at the maisonette, Aileen eyed the chair with a frown on her face. I was seeing it properly for the first time as well. It was a dead solid lump of furniture; all bare wood, darkened with age and chipped here and there from use. The backrest was firmly fixed on thick spars, and the legs were thick, with fancy bulges half-way down. It was like a cuckoo in our nest of stylish modern furnishings.

'Christ, what a deeply ugly thing that is,' I said.

Aileen didn't agree. She tilted her head to one side and said:

'Oh, I don't know; it's exactly the kind of chair I want in the kitchen when we get our cottage in the country. I'm not having any of your second-hand office junk that we've got here.'

What a time to drop a cottage in the country on my head. Leave that one for later, I thought. I went for the other part instead.

'Second-hand!' I said. 'That monstrosity must be fifth- or sixth-hand.'

'This is no time to start an argument,' she answered. 'Let's not burn our bridges till we get to them.'

My mouth was still hanging open when she went on:

'Right! Let's get down to business. Pick up that chair and shake it.'

It was like shaking a jumbo jet, except that it took us nowhere. I gave Aileen a questioning look that said, What next? She was thinking.

'Right!' she said. 'We'll have to take it apart. Start with the legs.'

Twenty minutes later I was sweating rivets, and all I had managed was to get one of the front legs off. It involved a lot of jumping on the spars between the legs, which failed to break them. I had to saw them off in the end. Once I had done that, there was no chance of putting a whole chair back in the container, so I shrugged and sawed a leg off flush with the underside of the seat. I handed it to Aileen. She waved it around for a moment.

'OK,' she said, by way of variation, 'cut off the top three inches.'

I sighed and did as I was told. Nothing.

Three cuts later my saw rasped on something that wasn't wood. So I carefully sawed in as far as the something all the way round the leg at that point. When I finished, the two parts of the leg slid apart, releasing an aluminium tube which was open at both ends. Aileen grabbed it eagerly.

'I knew it,' she yelled, and started to pull packing material out of the tube. Soon she had a little pile of jewellery on the table, and started checking items off on her list.

I was still busy being amazed at the leg. Even now that I had taken it apart, I couldn't tell where it had been cut, drilled, and put back together with the valuables inside. That William Somerville certainly was some kind of master craftsman.

Aileen interrupted my thoughts to tell me that she had accounted for about half of the items on the E26 list.

'Cut the other front leg in the same place. The rest of the jewellery must be there. The back legs are too thin.'

Suddenly she was an expert. But of course she was right as usual – there it was. And soon we had a little pile of shiny trinkets which were worth thousands of pounds, if you could believe the valuations on the list. Aileen was pawing through the stuff with an eager glint in her eyes, but I couldn't work up any enthusiasm.

'How do you like it?' Aileen asked. She was wearing a diamond necklace. To me it looked just like the ones you can buy for fifteen pounds in those shops that sell cheap costume jewellery in every shopping centre.

'Lovely,' I said. 'It really suits you ... but there's no way we can keep any of it.'

'Oh, I know,' she answered with a sigh. 'We have to hand it over to Neil – maybe there's a reward.'

I thought about that. I would have liked to keep it up our sleeves, but we would still have had to hand it in sometime. If there was any reward, it occurred to me that Senga should be in line for a share. Angus was just an unlucky prawn in the game who got caught in the crossfire. And I was lucky not to be in the same boat. I nodded wisely, to show Aileen I had considered all the possibilities.

'You're right – it's got to be handed over to Neil. Remember the cops and the Customs and Excise have never found anything. So we need the jewellery to convince him that we're telling the truth; and it's evidence as well.'

So the whole lot – the valuables and all Steve's printed lists – went into a Marks and Spencer plastic bag, which I put in my hidy-hole above the bathroom ceiling. I still hadn't thought of a better place to hide things.

The ruined chair was a problem. But I solved that by sawing it up into quite small pieces. I wrapped the bits in old newspapers and slipped out to dump them in Miss Downie's wheelie-bin, while Aileen hoovered up the sawdust. A bit like getting rid of a body, I suppose.

By that time it was about half-past three in the morning, so we dragged ourselves off to bed, grateful that we wouldn't have to get up and go to work in the morning, it being Sunday.

And we both felt as if we had done a good night's work.

20

We woke up bright and early on the Sunday morning; half-past nine in fact. Well, that was early considering what time we got to bed. By ten o'clock we felt ready to face Neil – on the blower at least. As it happened, it was Sally who answered the phone, and I wondered if she had moved in with Neil – on a permanent basis, I mean, rather than just the odd weekend.

'He's in the middle of shaving,' Sally said. 'I might as well have a word with Aileen while you're waiting.'

So Sally and Aileen went on for ages about where the best sales were and what a cow that Samantha in the hairdresser's was and what Aileen said to the customer who tried to chat her up and what she wished she had said – and would have if only she had thought of it at the time. It ended up with Neil at his end and me at my end, hanging around like a pair of right dooleys, waiting for the downpour to stop pouring down.

In the end I got to explain to Neil that we had found some important new evidence that he would very definitely be interested in. He sounded quite businesslike, and right away decided to come over to the maisonette.

'OK,' I said. 'See you when you get here.'

Aileen nudged me quite painfully with an elbow. She doesn't realise how sharp some of her body parts can be.

'Tell him to bring Sally,' she whispered.

I said into the phone, 'Aileen says bring Sally, even though they can't have anything left to say to each other.'

It was a good hour before they arrived, Neil breezing straight in with a bit too much confidence, I thought. While Aileen and Sally made for the bedroom to get on with some intensive frock stock-taking, he sat down on the sofa and said, 'Got some news for you, Kenny.'

I acted pretty cool, and just raised my eyebrows without

saying anything. Neil went on: 'I called the Metropolitan Police Department while I was waiting for Sally to get ready. They've pulled in Percival Hopper and Lionel Bickerstaff early this morning, charged with the murder of your mate Angus. It was that blasting cap that did it . . .'

He stopped and turned his head to look me straight in the eye. Butter wouldn't melt, I thought. Something changed in his expression and made him start his run-up again.

'Oh yes. You wouldn't know, but we found a blasting cap – a detonator – in the room Hopper occupied in the Shakespeare Hotel. His prints were on it . . . and Forensic have established it was the same type that was used to set off the charge in Angus's car.'

So that was how he wanted to play it. No hint of a thank-you. Not a shred of gratitude to me for handing him the Boss gang all neatly wrapped up like a Chinese takeaway. I bet this goes a long way towards getting Neil promoted.

Well, why should I care – I was just relieved to know that these nutters were locked away. Neil had more to tell me.

'I was able to tell the Met chaps what to look for when they searched our friend's "drums" – their word, not mine. They found that Bickerstaff's wardrobe had sprouted a brown overall with Lone Harp Auto printed across the back and a tab inside the neck that said "A Costello".'

Christ, one of Angus's own overalls. I suppose they were the only ones big enough for loathsome Lionel. Lucky he kept it, perhaps as a souvenir; or maybe he was just too thick to think of dumping it.

Anyway, I was getting pretty fed up with Neil's attitude. Dead smug, he was. You'd have thought he'd found a cure for the greenhouse effect. So I changed the subject.

'I've got something that might interest you,' I said. I had got the Marks and Spencer plastic bag containing the jewellery and the printouts out of the bathroom ceiling while Neil was on his way over. I didn't want him smirking knowingly while I took a chair into the bathroom and emerged with the goods.

I reached behind the sofa to pick up the M&S bag, and watched Neil smirk knowingly. I'm afraid that made me throw it at him with some force; but he was alert enough to catch it.

'What's this then?' he said, and then shut up as a diamond ring fell out and lay winking up at him from Aileen's Chinese rug.

So I let Neil in on the whole thing. What else could I do now that things had gone this far? For the first time I was holding nothing back, except for keeping Steve out of it. I just let Neil think that the printouts had somehow come from the Lone Harp Auto computers.

I was kind of surprised at the effect it had on me – you know, having no secrets left; well, hardly any. Leave Scheri out of this. It was a kind of freedom, getting rid of the responsibility – handing over the worry to somebody whose job it was to do something about it. I could see that Neil was pretty excited, the way he kept wading through the lists of furniture and jewellery. You'd have thought he had won the National Lottery.

'So there's a load of this stuff in the warehouse now, right?'

He looked up at me with raised eyebrows. I nodded and guided him to the famous list of furniture items where the numbers had an E in front of them.

'There's less ... fewer ... this list is shorter than the others. Why is that?'

I nearly said, use your bloody head, birdbrain; but remembered in time that Neil is not really a birdbrain, and anyway this was no time to get on the wrong side of the law. So I just told him that Scheri didn't put furniture on the list until it arrived in the warehouse and there was more stuff to come in the next few days probably.

Neil was still so hypnotised by the sparkly jewels and such that I wondered if I should risk asking him for a receipt. But of course they were itemised on the printout that went with the chair.

He was quiet for a while – just thinking, I suppose. Then he said:

'OK, you let me know when all the stuff has arrived. I'll make arrangements for a raid, and with your help we'll time it to swoop on Quinn when he's in the warehouse with the maximum amount of loot.'

'Wait a minute,' I protested, 'I'll likely be there as well. Quinn wants me to help him pack the container. I don't want to be collared in the confusion. I've never had anything to do with the jewellery-laundering racket. You know that.'

All I got was a nasty grin.

'You just leave it to me, Kenny. I'll make sure you come out of it smelling of roses. If we wait for the container to leave the warehouse it might get out of my patch before being stopped.'

He didn't say so, but it was obvious he was determined to get all the credit for himself. Well, it was too late for me to back out now. Besides, he had me by the balls. So that was how we left it. I would keep Neil informed about all the movements of antiques and people.

Eventually Neil went off all happy with Sally and his Marks and Spencer bag of goodies. Aileen and I were left at a loose end, not knowing what to do for the rest of Sunday. It had started to rain, so we didn't want to go out anywhere.

I had this heavy feeling in my stomach, with my brain cells thinking up dozens of ways things could go horribly wrong in the next week. No, it was worse; there was that heavy feeling of foreboding inside me. There had to be something I could do to take my mind off it; so what I did was, I got out my Black and Decker drill and got on with fixing up the pine bookshelves. At least I could earn some Brownie points from Aileen.

At Lone Harp Auto the next morning – that would be the Monday of that final week – everybody was in there, doing their various things. All except Quinn, which was interesting because it made me start wondering if he had sniffed a whiff of danger after Angus's murder, and decided to fade away before the cops could pick him up. Well, that's what I was kind of hoping, but my brain cells knew really that Quinn was so arrogant and greedy that he would never run out on a shipment of valuable jewellery. And he would never credit the police with enough sense to make any kind of case against him.

Quinn finally rolled in about eleven thirty, when I was in the back office having coffee with Scheri. The door suddenly flew open and there he was, hands held out from his sides as if he was the fastest gun in the West, ready to draw and fire in three micro-seconds. It was a bloody good thing he didn't have any six-shooters in his belt, I remember thinking. Not that he would have had any reason to fire. I mean Scheri and I were pretty close together but that was because we were going over a worksheet together for me to get familiar with how it was costed. We just turned our heads and stared at Quinn open-mouthed while he developed his Wyatt Earp act a bit more. The ends of his moustache quivered when he yelled:

'Piss off out of here, Madigan, back to the workshop where you belong. And in future you do your sniffing around after pussy in your own time – not while I'm payin' for it.'

I never said a word; just got up and went through Quinn's office to the workshop without even looking at him. That little bit of action was dead typical of Quinn, of course, and I'd got used to him being unpredictable. But this time my brain cells got their teeth around it and threw up a couple of things to think about. The first was that I never ever saw him yell directly at Scheri, though the results of his outbreaks often caused trouble and inconvenience for her. The second thing was that Scheri never got mad at Quinn; I mean, she was such a dominant character in every other situation, yet she just sat back and let Quinn have his own way, and never objected to his tantrums.

Anyway, later on Scheri let me know, just in passing like, that Quinn had only wanted to discuss some business matter with her in private. So he got rid of me in the first way that sprang to his mind. This seemed to be confirmed in the afternoon when Quinn called me into his office. He was all friendly nice as ninepins, as my Auntie Ursula would have said. Trouble is, Quinn scared me more when he was being nice than when he ranted at me.

'Are you rarin' to go, Kenny?' he said. 'I'll be needing your assistance this week, as we agreed.'

'OK,' I said, being careful not to nod or give any other sign of agreement or friendliness. I was determined to keep as much distance as I could between Quinn and myself. And to me that meant mental distance as well as space. It didn't cut any ice with Quinn, though. He puffed out these ridiculous chubby cheeks and said:

'Relax, Kenny-me-lad. You're talking to me as if I was a tree stump. Think about the bonus I'm going to pay you for this – on top of the overtime.'

It was the first I'd heard about a bonus. Not that it made any difference. I dragged my attention back to what he was saying.

'The rest of the crappy old antiques are arriving tonight. Me and the truck driver will unload the junk and that's about all there will be time for. So it'll have to be you helping me out on Tuesday and Wednesday.'

Quinn searched my face for some sign of enthusiasm. Not finding any, he thrust his face towards me and added slowly, as if he was talking to a retarded foreigner:

'That's tomorrow and the day after. Right! Go home and have a bite to eat after you power-down here. Just be back at the warehouse by seven thirty and we'll work our arses off till about midnight.'

'Right!' I said and got out of the office.

Bastard!

I spent the rest of the afternoon wondering how I could avoid being in the warehouse when the cops descended on it. Sure as hell I would be collared and charged if I was found red-handed doing criminal work. I didn't see how Neil could do much to help me there; he was only a sergeant after all. And an operation as big and important as this one must involve inspectors and superintendents and for all I know bloody admirals of the fucking fleet.

Of course I could forget to tell Neil what was going on, but then I would definitely be torpedoed by some of the biggest slings and arrows since 1066.

I was buggered if I did and buggered if I didn't.

So I did. Neil was anxious to get every detail, and made me repeat everything twice while he was obviously making notes at the other end of the phone. Finally he said:

'OK, here's what we'll do. I want to wait until most of the stuff is in the container – so we do it late on Wednesday. I'll arrange to have squad cars in position all round the Lone Harp site from about nine thirty – not too close, though.'

He went quiet for a bit. Always a bad sign with Neil, I had discovered. It usually meant he was thinking up some new worries for me. Finally he started talking again.

'What we really need is some kind of signal so we'll know when to move in.'

'Shouldn't be a problem for you,' I said, having a private guess that what was coming wouldn't be all that welcome. I acted dumb. 'You'll just shout *go-go-*GO into your radio thingie and feel like that copper on *NYPD Blue* and the sirens'll yodel and your rozzers will all rush in and club everybody to death including me.'

'That's not what I meant...' he started to say, and then realised I was winding him up. He tried again. Nicer this time, which made me even more suspicious, but it turned out I was misjudging him.

'Look, Kenny, I'm also trying to think of a way to get you out. How about if you give the signal? When the job's nearly done, you get out and run up the road in the opposite direction from the way out of the industrial estate. I'll fix it so I'm in the first car you'll come to. We'll crash in as soon as you pass my car. And you just keep on running – take the footpath out to Birmingham Road and stay clear. How does that strike you?'

Well, it sounded better than I'd hoped for. I felt quite encouraged for a change. How was I to know there was no chance of it happening like that?

Kenny Madigan the famous stupid pillock.

21

Tuesday night came and I turned up at the warehouse behind Lone Harp Auto as ordered by Quinn. He was there already, and so was Scheri. The rest of the antique furniture had arrived too. It was just a disorganised mass spilling forward from the back wall of the warehouse.

There wasn't much conversation, just sheer bloody hard work.

Scheri buzzed around dealing with the labelling and organisation of the items. She made notes and kept disappearing into the Lone Harp office to type the details into the computer. I wondered how she knew which pieces of furniture had valuables inside. I suppose she had the details of the jewellery already in the machine, but there had to be some way for her to know how it was allocated to the various antiques.

Anyway, I never found out. As I said, it was nothing but bloody hard graft for Quinn and me. I have to give him credit; he definitely wasn't work-shy. He worked like a maniac and expected me to do the same.

The way we went about it was like this. We first picked out a group of items that Scheri had finished numbering and labelling. Then we would get them up the ramp into the container any way we could. What I mean is, we would pick up lighter things such as chairs and small cabinets, and just carry them up into the mouth of the container.

That was the easy part; but there were a lot of enormous wardrobes, desks and sideboards. Some of these were so heavy that the two of us could only inch them slowly along the floor. We had to pick them up with one or other of the two forklift trucks and drive up the ramp into the container. Luckily most of the heaviest things had been put on pallets, I suppose so that they could be delivered here.

Once a group of furniture was inside, we had to pack them in tight, fill the container up to the ceiling, and secure them with ropes. This was the hardest part because there wasn't too much space for manoeuvring a forklift, so most things had to be manhandled into their final positions.

I could see now why it couldn't all be done in one night; not by two people anyway, not unless they were both Arnold Schwarzenegger. Quinn might have been helped by the Country and Western music blaring from the ghetto-blaster sitting on his forklift. It did nothing for me though.

So I was nearly dead on my feet by one o'clock in the morning when Quinn decided we had done enough for one night. I dragged myself out to my car and home to the snoring Aileen, knowing that I would have to go through the whole thing again the next night.

In the morning I wasn't too tired, considering. But every inch of my body was complaining. I had aches in muscles where I never even knew I had muscles as such – and it must have been obvious judging by the cracks the mechanics made about what kind of activities they thought I had been up to. If I'd had any choice I would have signed the pledge never to do any furniture moving for the rest of my life. Still, the aches gradually wore off and by the afternoon I was able to shuffle around the workshop almost like normal.

By the time I closed up Lone Harp Auto and went home for my dinner, my stiff muscles had taken a back seat in my mind. My brain cells were having a worry meeting about tonight being the day of reckoning. I had been kind of hoping that Wednesday would never come. But here it was. Aileen tried her best but she didn't make me feel any better when she gave me a parting hug and told me:

'Don't worry. In a few hours it'll be all over. By the way ... Sally told me Neil wants them to get married when he gets his promotion ... and that should come through as soon as he puts Quinn away.'

Bloody hell! Now I would get the blame for ruining Sally's wedding prospects if the Gestapo cocked up their raid on the warehouse. Well, I had plenty of more important things to worry about – like keeping my own skin out of all the shit that would be flying.

At first it was just the same as it had been the previous night, though I couldn't look at Quinn without thinking, Little do you know, mate ... you're for the chop.

But then I would remember Scheri, who had arrived with Quinn in his car although she had finished her labelling and cataloguing on the Tuesday night. She stayed in the Lone Harp Auto office, I suppose tending her computers and making sure everything was up to date. I couldn't help feeling guilty about having done nothing to warn her about the police raid. What would become of her? Scheri had never done me any harm ... quite the opposite, in fact. But there was no way I could prevent her being banged up for at least five years. I would just have to settle for being a heel and a traitor.

Quinn was locked into his working mode. Shuttling around expertly on a forklift truck with his ghetto-blaster belting out the usual Country and Western crap. We were getting through the work quite well, and we sort of fell into a routine ... you know, without planning it.

Quinn would decide on the size of the next group of furniture to be loaded. That really depended on how many items we could get into the mouth of the container and still leave room to work on packing them in and stacking them against the stuff that was already packed. Anyway, he would tell me something like:

'OK, we'll take up to one-twenty-three now.'

Then I would work on the ground, moving pieces to where he could pick them up with the forklift. I had taken to using a long crowbar as a lever to help me shift the heavier stuff the few inches needed to make it accessible. Then we had the nasty job of going inside the container to do the actual packing and stacking and securing with ropes.

By about ten thirty we were well through the job and took a breather. I looked around. There was only enough furniture left on the floor of the warehouse for about three more batches. It was mostly heavy stuff, all against the side wall, and didn't look like such a lot compared to what we had already shifted. But there was an old piano which we had kind of avoided up to now on account of it looked solid enough to build a lighthouse on.

I knew that Neil and the Seventh Cavalry would be in position outside by this time. Any moment now I could grab a chance to slip outside and give the signal for them to storm the quarry. To hell with waiting for everything to be loaded up. I said I was going for a pee and slipped out the big door.

No police.

Never trust a copper.

Back inside, Quinn sounded really friendly as he twitched that black moustache and grinned at me, saying:

'OK, my man. You and me have moved mountains here. Just one last bout of muscle work and you'll deserve everything that's coming to you.'

I should have been scared by then if I'd had any sense. At the very least I should have smelt a mouse. But I was thinking, one more batch and then when he goes into the container I'll make my move. The coppers must arrive soon and if they don't I'm out of here regardless. Quinn went on:

'Right! Let's go. We'll take a bunch out of the middle ... including the iron maiden there.'

He pointed to the piano. This was a change of tactics, because we had been taking our batches of furniture strictly in numerical order up to now. And still I never suspected dirty work at the

161

level crossing – my brain cells were busy being well choked over having to go the distance with that piano.

Kenny Madigan the well-known prize sucker.

Well, it was the same old routine. Soon most of the batch was in the mouth of the container and the only thing left was that piano flat against the wall. Although it had wheels they were just tiny things, they didn't have a cat in hell's chance of rolling on the uneven concrete of the floor.

I wrestled with it in the confined space, gradually levering one end out from the wall with my trusty crowbar until the bloody thing was at enough of a slant for me to squeeze round behind it. Then I pushed and levered at the other end until the sodding piano was straightened up, ready to be picked up by Quinn's forklift truck.

But I was still in the tight space behind it. There was bulky furniture – things like Victorian wardrobes and solid oak sideboards – on both sides of me. So I couldn't come out until Quinn lifted the piano on his forks and reversed out. Even then I had no reason to be worried.

I was living in an idiot's paradise.

Looking over the top of the piano I saw the forklift truck coming forward, its forks down near the floor. It stopped at the right place. The piano started to rise . . . and rise . . . and rise. It rose beyond the call of duty. Until it was as high as that truck could take it. About fifteen feet up.

I was waiting for the forklift to move backward. At last it did move – but forward. Towards me. Until the piano was against the wall again. Way above my naked head.

Right in front of my face, Quinn's twisted lips snarled down from the controls. He turned down the volume on his ghetto-blaster so I could hear him yelling:

'Asshole, nobody fucks with me and mine and gets away with it.'

I was thinking, OK, he's trying to scare me and he'll let me out in a minute. But I *was* getting a bit twitchy, what with the piano of Damocles hanging over me. People shouldn't lark about with dangerous things; that's how accidents happen.

Quinn was yelling at me again in that slow voice:

'It ain't enough for you to go shagging my personal pussy – you've got to go and rob me into the fucking bargain. I want to hear you plead for your life before I turn you into a heap of mush under this ton of rusty crap.'

Jesus Christ, I thought. He sounds as if he really means it.

The piano dropped ... about a foot – and I tried to burrow into the cement floor.

At last it penetrated my thick skull. The fucking maniac is dead serious. He is about to kill me. I replayed that: *He is about to kill me.*

Quinn's moustache quivered. He even looked to be enjoying himself.

I could smell my own sweat. Not much of it was caused by the physical work. I looked up. The brass plate on the bottom of the piano said 'Iron Frame, Overstrung'. I never did like heavy metal music. Fancy being killed by a percussion instrument. That's right, Kenny, think of another joke that could be your last thought. It might stop you emptying your bladder here and now.

I tried an appeal to his better nature but my voice was shaking as much as the rest of me:

'Come on, Quinn. Let me out and we ... we can discuss it like civi ... civilised people.'

Quinn's face was red now, and I could see a vein throbbing in his forehead:

'No chance, Asshole. If you hadn't thieved my gun, I could shoot you. As it is, you're going to die the hard way. Think of all I've done for you. Geez, I even killed a guy for kidnapping you.'

Bloody hell, no better nature, as such. The bastard really is a loony. He thinks I would rather be shot for a fish as a lamb.

How about an appeal to reason?

'They'll find my bod ... find me ... and come after you. You'll be nicked for ... murder.'

'Nah,' he said. 'I'll be well away from this dump before anybody thinks of looking for you in here. This load starts rolling first thing in the morning and I'm out of this god-forsaken hole for ever. I've got enough loot to retire now – and I don't give a shite what happens to Lone Harp Auto.'

A bloody regiment of coppers on the way and they're fucking useless. What's new? Desperation forced me to try again.

'I can shout for help. Someone might hear ... and ... they might get the police here in time to collar you.'

Pathetic, right? Quinn laughed again and said:

'Try shouting louder than Garth Brooks, Asshole.'

He turned the ghetto-blaster volume up to maximum. The whole warehouse was suddenly bristling with twanging guitars and a rabble of yelling voices. Quinn gave me a minute to enjoy the best his favourite music could offer.

His teeth were marble tombstones hanging out to dry.

I couldn't take my eyes off that sparkling set of teeth.

I was gripping my crowbar so tight my right hand was going numb.

The crowbar!

Maybe . . .

But his hand was hovering too close to the lever that would release the forklift's hydraulic pressure and send the piano crashing down on me. I watched that hand and chose my moment when it moved further away.

I whipped the crowbar up and made as if to launch it like a javelin towards Quinn's neck.

He was expecting that. He laughed out loud as he swayed sideways to let it fly past. The one time he got it wrong. I never threw the crowbar.

You know when you pretend to throw a stick for a dog to fetch and the poor beast chases nothing. It was like that with Quinn dodging the crowbar. For about two seconds he didn't know what was happening. Maybe he was waiting to hear the crowbar clang to the concrete behind him.

Somehow, without needing to think about it, I knew what to do. I snicked the Y gap at the far end of the crowbar on to one of the control levers of the forklift, just under the knob at the top of the lever. Praying I'd picked the right one, I pushed with the crowbar. The lever notched back, towards the rear of the truck. Which lurched backwards.

It *was* the right lever.

I was out of my prison like shit off a hot shovel as soon as a big enough gap opened up. Quinn grabbed his end of the crowbar and I let him keep it, in the interests of getting my valuable body out from under the piano.

My life expectancy had improved. But not by all that much. Quinn was between me and the door, which was closed. And now he was swinging his forklift round to come after me, the devil's piano still swaying aloft. I ran towards the back of the warehouse with the idea of getting round the other side of the container where there was more space. Quinn cut me off by going round his end of the container.

Seeing I was cornered, Quinn took a moment to dump the piano, before coming after me again. That gave me time to climb on to the other forklift truck which was parked against the back wall to be out of the way.

Now I was mounted too. I drove the truck towards the door only to be intercepted. And again. These forklift trucks are not fast but they are very heavy because of being counterweighted, so they pack a lot of mass. When two of them collide, they do so with a sickening thud that jars its way through your whole body. Quinn wasn't going to let me get past him, so it was like a couple of dodgem cars bumping to try and dislodge each other from the saddle.

I tried again. This time I swerved to the right at the last moment in an attempt to get past. But of course he swerved left so that we were running parallel. That was when the evil bastard swung the crowbar at my head. My left arm went up to protect me and took the full force of the blow. I knew right away that it was broken, though I hardly felt a thing at the time.

There hadn't been time to be scared since I got on the forklift truck. But now the idea got through to my brain cells that I would soon be dead – unless I did something . . . I could still drive my dodgem with one hand. I continued turning right to complete the circle and stopped facing Quinn again. The bastard was waiting for my next charge. Garth Brooks was silent now, the ghetto-blaster having smashed to the concrete floor in one of our collisions. My diabolical boss brought out most of his teeth again. He waved the crowbar and yelled:

'Next time it's your head, Asshole.'

Bloody hell, it's *High Noon*, I thought. I moved forward for the final showdown.

I did the same as last time, starting a swerve to the right. But straightened up with Quinn repeating his left turn. Then I let the steering look after itself while my right hand used the control that works the forks. His truck was more or less broadside on when I reached it. The first contact was the right prong of my forklift crunching into Quinn's side, just before the jarring impact of the two trucks. Quinn shifted sharply away from me and landed on the floor.

He didn't move.

I sat there taking a few deep breaths. Empty of everything except the big lump of lead where my intestines used to be before they crawled away to safety.

Then Scheri was there, helping me down. Stupidly the main thought in my mind was a worry about being able to find a new job with a broken arm.

'Are you OK, honey?' she said. 'I came in a couple minutes ago but there wasn't a goddam thing I could do.'

I didn't hear her, being too busy concentrating on not passing out. I was grateful to Scheri for holding on to me till the nasty moment was over.

Thank you, Scheri; you're wonderful.

Once some of my body's functions had got back up to limping-along level, I thought, What about Quinn?

'What about Quinn?' I said.

We bent over the crumpled lump on the ground. I wouldn't have touched him for a night with Pamela Anderson (but maybe for a gulp of whisky, at that moment). Scheri was quite matter-of-fact, though.

'Shattered rib-cage,' she announced. 'The prong of that there forklift was just the right height to make gumbo out of his innards. He had it coming.'

'So he's dead, then?'

I hadn't meant that to happen, but was surprised to find no regrets in me. For some reason I was more concerned about coming to terms with this new callous version of Scheri.

'Yup,' she said. 'The end of a long and filthy career. And I'm free from him at long last.'

Astounded was not a strong enough word for what I felt. My mouth was hanging open, but I managed to ask:

'What was the hold that Quinn had over you? Was it blackmail or something?'

Scheri nodded and looked kind of sad.

'Not blackmail exactly . . . Something.'

Then she put her arms round me, being careful not to touch my useless left arm. She smiled at me but with what looked like a tear added to the sadness in her eyes. Her voice went husky when she said:

'You're a sweet innocent guy, Kenny. Promise me you'll always stay that way. And remember me sometimes.'

I waited in that warehouse for as long as I could stand it. After a while I wandered outside to meet the police force. They still weren't there.

Never *ever* trust a copper.

My brains were not working well enough to help me decide on anything to do, so I walked off to the side and sat down in the dirt to wait for whatever might come along. I definitely was not going back into that warehouse.

Ten minutes later five cars arrived in a cloud of sirens and flashing blue lights. They swung round the Lone Harp Auto building and screeched to a stop, with all their headlights blazing on the warehouse door. Uniforms and plain-clothes coppers erupted from every car door and stood around like a bunch of condoms at an orgy – ready for action but not sure what they'll be asked to do.

Neil was in the middle of it, officiously spreading out his men. I sighed and started towards him, holding my broken left arm which was hurting like hell by this time – and limping badly.

There was nothing wrong with my leg. But I thought I *deserved* a limp.

22

Isn't it amazing how fast things happen? Here I am, my left arm still in plaster from that diabolical night at Quinn's antiques warehouse, and it's a whole different world.

Mind you, it all looked a bit dicey for a while. I've got to admit that. The coppers kept talking to me for a long time, and even Neil was acting as if it was hard to believe my story. What do I mean, *even* Neil; *especially* Neil would be more like it. You would have thought he would be dead sympathetic, what with him

167

knowing all the background and all. Not to mention me suffering
agonies from my broken arm. For him the arm was just a bloody
nuisance that delayed me being grilled until the hospital did
some repairs on me. Still, at least I had the presence of mind to
go into a dead faint that night when the rozzers started getting
too inquisitive.

See, they had this problem about how Quinn met his end. Neil
seemed to think my story was a bit vague. As if I would be
taking careful notes while some lunatic is trying to kill me.
Anyway, he kept on and on at me with stuff like:

'Was he a tall man . . . the one driving the other forklift truck?
You must have been pretty close to him when he broke your arm
with the crowbar. And then you just stood watching while he
and Quinn fought it out on forklift trucks? It all sounds a bit far-
fetched to me. What was he wearing?'

And I would wrinkle my brows trying to remember, and shake
my head from side to side.

'The only thing I know for sure is the tights he had over his
head. Oh, and the motor-cycling gloves, of course.'

Neil was on to that right away, checking his notes.

'Come on, Kenny; make up your mind. Ten minutes ago you
said it was a stocking over his head.'

That's the kind of nit-picking he was reduced to. I tried to be
patient and helpful.

'Stocking – tights – what's the difference? Anyway, I suppose
he was quite a big man. I couldn't even tell you what colour he
was. On account of the . . . stocking, that is.'

I brightened up a bit at that thought.

'Hey, maybe that's it. It could of been the ghost of Angus come
back to save me.'

Neil gave up in disgust, though I'm sure he still thought I
wasn't giving him the whole truth. I don't know why they
wouldn't just take it at face value; after all, they had smashed
one of the biggest fencing rackets ever, all thanks to me. You'd
think some gratitude would not be out of place.

I didn't expect it, but I got the last laugh over the matter of the
mysterious stranger who saved my life by killing Quinn. Neil
was called away from one of these sessions where I was being
grilled. He came back looking pretty thoughtful and told me:

'OK, Kenny. I still don't believe you but I think I'm going to have to try. I just heard that your old mate Lionel Bickerstaff had it away from our friends of the Metropolitan Police Department ... Inefficient bastards ... Anyway, if we decide to believe you, it could be that Bickerstaff came here with the idea of getting revenge on Quinn.'

I never heard whether poor old Lionel got picked up again, and I didn't really give a bugger. If he was, he must have felt even more stupid than usual at some of the questions he would have been asked.

There were still some entrails hanging in the air though. For instance, they never did find Scheri. See, any time the coppers find a dead body – especially a murdered one – they start babbling about scene-of-crime teams and incident rooms and pathologists and for all I know, astrologists. All this excitement tends to distract them. So it was longer than it should have been before they got around to checking Quinn and Scheri's shared bungalow in Snitterfield.

When they finally got there it was empty. They never worked out how Scheri knew it was time to scarper. Anyway, her car was gone, and they found nothing odd – except a folding bicycle lying outside the front door.

Good old Ergo.

Scheri's car was found abandoned about ten days later – in Dublin of all places – with false plates on. I got this from Neil much later. She didn't turn up in her old haunts in Texas and was never tracked down by the authorities on either side of the ocean.

One thing I kept away from Neil was about that place in Alcester. You know, where I was imprisoned for a night and where we found Mozzer's body. Who knows when I might need some information up my sleeve. Besides, after all I had been through, I thought it would be a good idea not to offend all the criminal bigwigs in the Midlands.

The only good thing that came out of it all was the reward. An awful lot of stolen jewellery was rescued, and the insurance companies were suitably grateful. Apparently they have a standard rate of reward based on the valuation of recovered goods. Anyway, the reward came to Aileen and me. It seemed like an awful lot of money. And it *was* a lot of money, though not enough to make me feel that the whole sodding thing was worth it.

Aileen and I had a board meeting about the reward money and we agreed to share it with Senga on account of she came off worst of all the good guys (except Angus of course, but there was nothing we could do for him).

For once everything fell into place. The receivers came in to Lone Harp Auto and let it keep ticking over while they examined the books with a view to disposing of the business or selling off its assets. After quite a lot of prodding from Aileen, I broached the receivers to see what the chances were of buying the company.

You could have knocked me over with a tyre-lever when I realised that we had enough dosh to become the new owners. I had squirrelled away most of the proceeds of my car-nicking career and what with that and the reward money, Aileen and I could buy ourselves into a lifetime of worry and responsibility.

Not exactly what I craved for, as such. But Aileen insisted that it would be a steady source of income, so in the end I settled for becoming a boss. I just hoped I wasn't jumping out of the frying pan into the melting pot.

Kenny Madigan the capitalist fat cat.

We offered Senga the chance to invest her share of the reward money in a slice of Lone Harp Auto, and she agreed on condition that she could have a job there after her baby was born. This confused me a bit at first because I thought she wanted to do the accounting and paperwork, but Senga explained that, being a hotshot mechanic, she wanted Angus's old job – foreman in the workshop ... or I suppose I should say forewoman – or foreperson.

'Wait a minute,' I said, 'we came over here to do you a favour, and now you're laying down the conditions for accepting it. Anyway, I'm the foreman.'

'Shut up, Kenny.'

That was Aileen – being bossy again. Then she turned to Senga.

'Take no notice of what Kenny says. He just hasn't thought it through yet. As proprietor of Lone Harp Auto, he won't have time to take care of every detail of running the workshop. He'll need a full-time foreman.'

I couldn't take that sitting down.

'Senga,' I said, 'you told us you can't drive. You can't have a job in a workshop if you're not able to move cars around at a moment's notice.'

'Ach!' she said. 'I'm an expert driver. I just havenae got a licence. If it makes ye feel better Ah'll take a driving test.'

Aileen stepped in then.

'Right, that's settled then. You've got your new foreperson – after the baby arrives.'

I couldn't quite put my finger on it, but somewhere along the way I must have made the decision.

Oh well, I wouldn't want to be seen biting the hand that rocks the cradle.

We spent some time admiring the Sydney Opera House. Senga had kept her promise to finish it. I remember thinking it was more Angus than the urnful of dust that came out of the crematorium.

So what with one thing and another, I suppose things are really looking up for Aileen and me, or at least they will be once the plaster comes off my left arm. As it is, I can't drive anywhere, so Aileen has to take me any time I need to go any distance.

I'm still supervising the Lone Harp workshop every day, in spite of my handicap. Got to protect my investment while I'm waiting for the paperwork to go through and the lawyers to get even richer. Brian Miller, my new mechanic – he picks me up on his way to work every morning, and drops me off at night.

It's Saturday today, and Aileen is at work (still in the Jonathan Phillips shoe shop; she enjoys it too much to leave and anyway she's got none of the skills she would need to do any job at Lone Harp Auto), so I took a walk into the town. Just having a look around the shops, you know. When I got back there was the usual pack of kids kicking a ball around on the rough grass behind the maisonettes, and it occurred to me that it wouldn't be long before Miss Downie came out to shout abuse at them. That would be worth seeing, I thought.

So I wasn't expecting to see a wheelie-bin rolling slowly down the slight slope of the passage between the buildings, with a pair of legs sticking out of it. Better than finding a hand in a car boot, but not something you see every day, as such. At least these legs were alive; they were trying to tread air, and I could hear a muffled voice complaining from the depths of the bin.

I stood in front of the runaway to stop its gentle progress.

'What are you doing in there?' I asked, peering down inside it.

'I was giving it a damn good scrubbing,' Miss Downie said and went on to explain:

'Aliens has been puttin' their rubbish in my wheelie-bin of late and I don't want to catch none of their germs. I must have overbalanced what with tryin' to reach my scrubber down to the bottom.'

I was trying to take it seriously, so I couldn't say much in case I would laugh. After a while I managed a lame comment:

'You should have laid it on its side first.'

'Well, I'll know that next time,' she said, quite nippy-like.

There was another pause and then she went on:

'Could you help me get out of here? My sister Daisy had to have her hysterectomy all taken away after she sat in a French bus for a week.'

This was a bit of a problem. I said:

'Oh, sorry . . . See, I've still got this broken arm and there's no way I could manage with one hand.'

So I shouted for the gang of kids to come and help. They soon had her the right way up, and by the time I was putting the key in my own front door, Miss Downie was inviting them all in to her maisonette for lemonade and Kit-Kats.

That's about as much excitement as I want to get my back teeth into from now on.